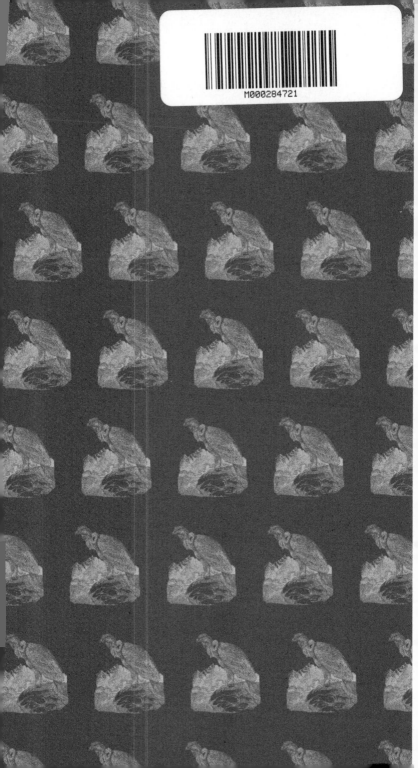

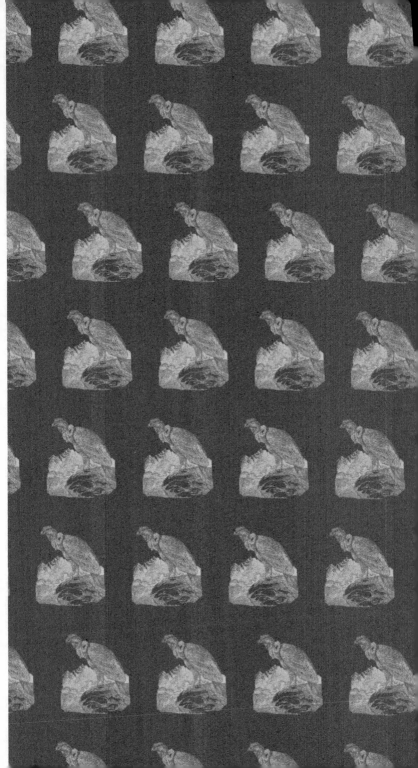

To Be Devoured

Sara Tantlinger

Apocalypse Party

Book Design by Mike Corrao
Cover Design by Matthew Revert

Paperback: 978-1-954899-09-4

Introduction

"**O**ur deaths deserve no other meaning than to be devoured." These words stuck with me long after reading them in the pages of this novella. Last year, when I painted my office red with silhouettes of black crows adorning the walls, it didn't take long for me to decide on a literary quote to accompany these timeless symbols of death. In black cursive against a crimson backdrop, the quote hangs above my door and suggests that there is no other purpose for our deaths other than to become sustenance for something else. It's a morbidly bleak take on death which echoes throughout the story.

Sara Tantlinger's mastery of poetic prose helps create a blended tapestry of both beauty and gore, and it is difficult to distinguish one from the other as they are stitched together with seamless delicacy.

The characters are written with expert care, so that the reader can see the beauty of the macabre through the eyes of the protagonist, Andi. I felt her pain, her traumas, her loss. Andi is written so well that the reader can easily climb into her mind and wonder alongside her what carrion meat might taste like—albeit gagging at the thought. My stomach churned and my face soured at some parts, but my reader brain was content to blindly follow Andi in her exploration of the grotesque obsession.

There is some commentary out there about the "gross out scene" in this book, and I suppose there are technically a few of them. However, none of those scenes are gratuitous. Tantlinger withholds when necessary and dives into the visceral, full-fledged horror when the story requires. Those scenes are certainly memorable, and absolutely necessary to the plot as the protagonist unravels, but there is so much more beyond those gruesome moments.

There is imagery and symbolism. The use of color and metaphor. Expertly executed literary devices make *To Be Devoured* a book that balances—no, it doesn't just balance—it *dances* upon the imaginary line drawn between literary and genre horror. It should be taught in classrooms for the narrator's journey alone. It should be explored for its use of symbolism—the colors green and black and how they relate to light and dark, life and death, and the dynamics of Andi and Luna's relationship.

To Be Devoured was nominated for a Bram Stoker Award, and rightfully so. It has quickly become one of my favorite reads of all time.

Sara Tantlinger has created something truly special here. Many people finish this book in one sitting, ferociously flipping pages until they've reached the very end, gravid and traumatized by what they've ingested. Much like the coveted raw flesh which the protagonist longs to consume, this book was written with a similar purpose.

It was written…to be devoured.

Red Lagoe

"In what distant deeps or skies

Burnt the fire of thine eyes?

On what wings dare he aspire?

What the hand, dare seize the fire?"

—William Blake, "The Tyger"

1

Something is dead over there, hidden among the tall trees separating my property from Mr. Landon's. Between our homes rests a football field-sized strip of land, lifeless and brown from the December days. The early hour stretches on outside, morphing periwinkle clouds into buttery tones of the rising sun.

They don't stop circling the trees; those poor, ugly, bastardized versions of birds. "Bird" doesn't seem like the right term. Birds eat insects, seed and grain—the turkey vultures feast on marbled strips of the deceased. It's easy to picture their bald, red heads and ivory beaks spearing into the bloated body of a cow or whatever else decays in the woods.

Luna's sleepy mumbles pull me away from the window. Her body slumbers in peace while I place a gentle kiss on her warm cheek before disappearing from the bedroom. Excitement jitters through my chest as I navigate my way into the basement where her surprise waits.

A few summers ago, these beautiful, bright green moths took up residence on the outside of Mr. Landon's barn. He said they were called Luna moths, so I spent my days yearning to understand their lifespan and smooth, dusted patterns. How could I gift them to my own Luna?

The seasons turned colder; sometimes the internet is a wonderful place, and I was able to order Luna moth eggs. The big, plastic fish tank where the eggs turned to caterpillars proved to be a sustainable home. A few caterpillars didn't make it, but dozens survived after I fixed the temperature in the basement and kept the shelter sprayed with mist to maintain the humidity.

The shed skin of the caterpillars sits in a glass jar near the tank. It isn't part of Luna's gift, but throwing away the husks that once sustained each beautiful moth seemed too callous. Metamorphosis of the most recent batch happened four days ago. The adult Luna moths won't live much longer. Such short lifespans for such magnificent creatures.

Their silky, lime-green wings lie on the bottom of the tank between white oak sticks. With a careful hand, I collect the dead moths and secure the screen back over the remaining live ones. Luna's present is almost done, so I won't even need to wait for the rest to die.

Across the tank on a wooden table rests my artwork—an elegant, sewn collage of moth wings for my Luna. The pieces are so delicate to work with, and I can only touch the edges or else the patterns will tatter and ruin. Thread the color of key lime pie holds the portions together in a distorted shape. Old moths merge to create a pair of larger wings. They're too delicate to stitch on any more pieces. This pair would suit a young child more than an adult, but they are still so striking. Almost as beautiful as my Luna.

Basement lights reflect off the emerald green, and particles of dust swirl through the air as I carry the masterpiece upstairs.

"Andi?" Luna calls from the kitchen. Fresh brewed coffee wafts through the house and entices me into the kitchen where Luna sits at the table. Her raven curls are pulled back into a messy bun. She sees me peek around the corner and her face breaks into a cheery smile. The warm hazelnut tones of her skin glow from the stretches of early morning sunlight yawning in through the bay windows.

Soft wings brush my arm from where I hold them behind my back. "I have a present for you."

"What for?" she asks but her eyes light up. The coffee mug is left forgotten on the table as she moves nearer.

My shoulders shrug. "Well, I have that new appointment today, and you've been so supportive. I wanted to show my thanks by giving you something as beautiful as you."

Her cheeks flush as she smiles. "Love you, Andi."

"Love you, Luna-bug. Now close your eyes and hold out your hands but be careful because this is really delicate."

"Okay." Dark eyes close and her smooth hands stretch out with palms up. Anticipation sends my heart into frantic beats. With gentle fingers, I navigate the stitched quilt of wings onto her open palms. More green dust dances through the dim kitchen and sticks to both our clothes.

"It's so light! Can I open my eyes?"

My lips stretch into a pleased smile. "Yes."

Luna looks down at the wings in her hands. Her grin slowly morphs into an open-mouthed expression of revulsion.

"What the hell? Are these…real?"

Static clicks in my brain, trying to compute the situation. Heat rushes into my face. "Of course."

She yelps as if she'd just stepped on a bee and throws the wings toward me. They cascade lightly onto the floor before I can pluck them from the air. Half of a wing tears off from Luna's throw and emerald dust billows like a sooty vapor.

"I'm sorry," she whispers, looking between me and the mess on the floor. "It's a bunch of dead bugs, Andi." Her face distorts in disgust.

My teeth clamp around the insides of my cheeks, as if I can gnaw and bleed away the hurt of her refusal. Silently, I nod and gather the wings up. Luna says something in the background, but the words blur together.

"I love you, but…you focus on the weirdest things sometimes."

Luna leaves while I'm in the shower, but she placed a sweet apology note on my pillow, saying she'd go get lunch for us by the time I'm back from my session. I love her too much to stay mad, but the raw sting of rejection keeps pulsating in my brain, reminding me of all the time and attention I put into taking care of the eggs, the caterpillars, the moths—of cautiously stitching everything together to give my own Luna a set of wings.

The wings live on in secret in my basement. After all that care, throwing them away would be disrespectful. As I get dressed, I give each moth whose sacrifice went into the collage of wings a small burial in my mind where my brain is already riddled with tombstones. Each grave marker nothing more than a symbol of solid pain, constantly digging broken concrete slabs deeper into my head, reminders of all the funerals I've attended in my nearly three decades of life.

"Stop it," I say to no one. A mild chill encircles the room. Hardwood floors bounce the cold back at me as if to say, *we don't want your frost and your death, keep it away.*

The soft flesh of my arms cradles the snowed-over memories, forces them back inside to the darkest attic corner of my brain. They stay rooted there in sticky cobwebs until my therapist pulls them free, like a spider knocking away the remnants of dead bugs.

At least that's how my old therapist maneuvered bad parts around. What will this new Dr. Fawning do? If I don't talk to someone, all the sour fury inside my marrow builds up. An old doctor from my teenage years told me I'm in the gray area of suicide, meaning I contemplate it often, but most likely won't pull the trigger or drive my car into a river. I loved my parents, but don't want to follow in their footsteps to an early death. Freedom is all I want, to shift

14

my spine and shoulder blades like tectonic plates and grow wings instead. Fly, fly away...

After bundling up to face the early morning, I step outside and let the brisk air finish waking me up. Overhead, a kettle of vultures circles the expanse of field while another group rests in the bare branches of winter's trees. All the beautiful leaves are gone, having long fell victim to the freezing nights from earlier this month. Today, however, promises sun and slight warmth because it's Pennsylvania and the weather is indecisive, even in December.

Ugly birds drift in slow, lazy circles, but I shouldn't judge for what is simply in their nature. Every body is a waiting carcass to them, a future meal to be enjoyed—they don't care about aesthetics. They take care of it, strip away the decayed flesh from bones like a ravenous, sacred obligation, sharing the duty with pulsating maggots and buzzing flies. A voracious feast of the dead, purging rot and liquified tissue from the skeleton until advanced decay claims everything, giving the remaining nutrients back to the soil, to nature. The way Mother Earth intended. Nothing wrong about it.

Before she died, my last therapist told me I must confront what I've internalized about my own "perceived wrongness." She understood what it is to be a woman and how to come to terms with your own sense of wrong, what society deems wrong about you—wrong nose, wrong tits, wrong thighs, voice, mannerisms...

The carrion birds are survivors; they'll outlast us all, thriving long after any apocalypse. Envy sends a hot jolt through my stomach for both the birds and their dead meals. The body is never wrong for them. They devour it. They just eat. They are ugly, and I cannot blame them for this, cannot fault their design the way society faults mine, faults us all.

But today I move forward, inhaling the earthy scent of Dr. Fawning's office, as if dozens of woodsy candles and wall plug-ins are alive around us. She settles in across the room and stares with an unblinking gaze. Her eyelashes are thick as a black forest, and her irises are the deep brown soil beneath. Silent encouragement settles in the air like a welcoming hug from an old friend.

A deep breath rises in my lungs. "Guess I'll start?"

Quiet. A polite smile.

"My story always feels the same. I mean, it's what I told my last therapist before she…"

There exists a horrible ache below my ribs from where I miss her. She was the last person I really trusted, the last person who felt like family besides Luna, but cancer doesn't give a damn who you trust; it just takes away, eats up a person without giving anything back to the earth. No purpose, no place in the ecosystem—a giver of pain and nothing more. And now she is there in my brain's forest of tombstones.

What if scientists could shrink the vultures into incredibly miniature beings, tiny as bacteria? Maybe we could place them into our bodies, have them fly through our bloodstreams, our veins, our bones, our organs, our everything. Have them soar through and clean out all the bad parts—the cancer, the tumors, the buildup of what will one day bring our fleshy husks down into the unloving dirt.

What a strange, marvelous thing it would be. Eat away the bad parts—for me, eat away my sadness, the sticky, bitter feelings with their rage inside my body, cloying my will to live some days. Most days.

A strangled cough erupts in my throat. "I hate winter. Every year, every tiny fucking snowflake reminds me. I drove past the elementary school the other day and saw those kids building a snowman. All so friggin' happy."

Dr. Fawning twitches. It's a slight movement, but the glassy expression in her eyes tells me she's about to ask, *and how does that make you feel?*

"Pissed off," I answer the silent question. "And I know it shouldn't. Not everyone has dead little brothers. Life isn't fair, you know?"

Dr. Fawning still says nothing, but the wind howls outside and she nods her head slightly. Quiet. Polite.

"And then what my father did…It was like we were cursed. Or maybe I'm the cursed one since…" My voice dies into a whisper. "Since I'm the only one left. And my mother, I miss her so much."

My tongue becomes too heavy, like a dried onion bulb stuffed into the back of my throat. Enough sharing for today.

The rest of our time blurs by, but she listens better than anyone, maybe even better than Luna.

The harsh wind blows a chill through my coat and layered shirts when I leave. My hatred for winter remains as strong now as it did thirteen years ago. There's danger beneath the false purity of snow. Death in the speared points of icicles and frozen lakes. All of this cold, it never deserved my mother. She was brilliant, bright as a Shasta daisy, faking her attempts at happiness all those years after my brother died. When those daisies pop up now, I have to blink away scarlet stains on white petals. Always.

All the therapy I attended, all the medications I endured, none of it filled the vacancy left inside me from losing her. They are all here, my family and more, buried deep in my brain, trying to save me from the desire to fall, to drown, to bleed.

My palm strikes hard against my left cheek. Pain and heat. A slight ring in my ears as I drive.

Do not dwell in graveyards. Do not dwell in graveyards.

Hot air blows from the car vents, warming my fingers on the still-cold steering wheel. Outside the windshield, beyond the reflection of my cloudy face, the vultures mark the gray sky like a connect-the-dots game. A shudder dances through my spine as the car moves beneath the circling scavengers. Mr. Landon's property

17

is before mine, but hopefully he's busy tending to cows or doing whatever he does in his barn.

My car creeps forward down the dirt and gravel road, too low to the ground to press the gas any harder without risking a nasty scrape. The old farmer emerges from the barn and waves at me as he walks toward the driveway.

"Shit." My foot presses the brake and I roll the passenger window down. Strong traces of hay and cow manure drift in with the wind. Polite Fake Smile mode switches on. Landon isn't a bad man, it's just there are simply so many conversations about farm animals and the winter weather forecast a girl can take.

We're the only two out this far in the woods, isolated by a circle of trees connecting our driveway to the main road. Now I haunt my family's old house, more of a ghost than my mother or brother, or even my father, ever could be. I don't have enough money to leave, and I have come to take comfort in the familiar surroundings. There is always a song here—the cicadas of summer, hooting owls in the fall, and coyotes howling in the dead of winter.

There's comfort in Mr. Landon, too. He always looks the same—thick, snowy white hair. Even thicker glasses. He looks like the kind of man who was very handsome once, probably with dark hair and light eyes. He smiles, revealing a strong set of teeth and dimples that blend in with his other lines, like a great wrinkled bug. Big eyes blink at me with suspicion.

"What are you up to, Miss Andi?" His voice harbors a slight Tennessee lilt despite the decades he's been in Pennsylvania.

Polite Fake Smile wavers. "Just coming home from a drive, Mr. Landon." The old man doesn't need to know all my business.

"Cows are restless this morning," he continues, as if I asked. "Winter storm's gonna roll in."

"Ah. Well, I'll let you get back to work."

He waves my words away like they're gnats. "About lunchtime

for me. You want some gravy and biscuits?"

"No, thank you. I have plans with Luna." My grip tightens around the steering wheel.

"Yep, saw that red car of hers go up the drive earlier."

Thanks, eagle-eye. You friggin' watcher of all.

"If you girls get hungry, walk on down. I made plenty. Have to with my appetite." He chuckles and pats his stomach, which isn't nearly as pudgy as I'd expect from someone who eats like he does. "Before my old lady passed on, she used to look me straight in the eye and say, 'Henry, you're gonna eat yourself to death one day. You glutton!'"

He wags his finger through the open window and the whiff of damp hay strengthens. "That's still my sin. Nothing like a home-cooked meal, but if you're gonna have a sin, I say gluttony is the best one." He winks, like we're sharing a good inside joke.

A forced laugh rasps itself out of my dry throat.

"What about you?"

"What about what?"

The good-natured smile on his face gets replaced by a darker grin. "What's your sin?"

"Oh…" I trail off. My answer turns to a dawdling *uhmm* as the question catches me off guard. He can't mean Luna. Landon's old, but he's never shown us any hate. "My mom used to say I had the sin of wrath in me. She wasn't wrong."

He squints and leans forward so his head protrudes through the open window. "Wrath. You gotta watch that one."

"Right." Our eyes meet. "Well, I'm going to go. Take care."

"You too, Miss Andi." He lingers for a moment and then backs away, but there's no hesitation in me to roll up the window and drive. *Jesus.*

For a moment I almost considered telling him, but the cold way he looked at me changed my mind. My mother and I were alike

19

in many aspects, but her depression was quiet and hidden, softly bubbling beneath her surface. Mine was more active, more vengeful. During these times, I felt more like the daughter of wrath itself rather than my mother's child.

After my brother's death, I beat the shit out of anyone in school who said anything about him. One wrong look, one twisted joke about him landing like a potato sack on the ground, about my parents being too stupid to watch their own child, and I flew at my victim like a winged tiger, baring my teeth and going for the jugular. My mother understood my rage, but she made me change schools after I slashed a girl's forearm with an X-ACTO knife in art class. Four years later, my parents were dead. A nearby aunt took me in until graduation, but I did not speak to my peers and told myself to be content in my loneliness.

And then there was Luna.

This morning was far from ideal, but my heart commands to put the incident behind me and to look forward to seeing my girl again. We've been through too much already. Maybe she'll change her mind about the wings—there's always hope.

Small rocks ping against the undercarriage of my car as it lurches up the road. Vultures swerve through the sky, flying and then hunching down in the trees. Something is dead over there, or at least dying. Whatever it is, I don't want to know.

No more wrath for today. No more death.

2

I first met Luna three years ago while bartending at Rex's. The owner liked me well enough until anger got the best of me. One night I was taking the trash out when a girl's cries caught my attention. Her pleas for someone to leave her alone echoed around the brick alleyway.

"Calm down, sweetheart," came a slurred, drunken reply. Around the corner a massive dude had a ballerina-sized girl cornered and crying. He smacked one hand around her mouth and tore a long rip up the side of her thin dress. My hand tightened around the trash bag pressed to my side. The smooth rim of a dark green beer bottle poked its way through the too-full plastic. I stretched the bag open. Old nacho cheese and stale beer trailed through the air, making my nose wrinkle. Once retrieved, I launched the empty bottle toward the dude's back, thinking it would bounce off his big body and smash on the ground. The glass shattered.

He whipped around and screamed the furious howl of a wounded, drunk man. The cuts shone from the back of his neck where blood glittered like black water in the night. If only the bottle had split him open entirely and left him bleeding to death in the alley.

It at least distracted him enough for the girl to get away and for the bar's owner to call the cops. The girl thanked me. Rex's owner fired me for attacking a patron.

Luna was friends with the ballerina, and she rushed across the dimly lit bar.

"Hey, you saved my friend," she had said. Her indigo lipstick smeared against her teeth, but Christ was she beautiful. "My husband knows someone who could fix this. Want us to make a call? He has some great lawyer friends—"

"No worries, really." I held up a hand and waved away the kindness. "This place isn't worth it. There are other bars and other assholes out there to work for."

Even though I didn't drink much myself, I was a damned good bartender. My bookshelf overfilled with drink recipes, mixology guides, and lessons about the different reactions of alcohol, mixers, and flavors. Bartending turned into an artwork to pay the bills.

At the bar, I became somebody else and could pretend to be a normal woman for the night, earn my tips with good drinks and fake flirtations.

The wrath inside me, however, made me stay away from doing it again. There are only so many times you can watch the sleaze of the world ruin these girls who seemed, like me, to be fighting their own perceived wrongness. For weeks after, fantasies plagued me about smashing open the creep's head and choking him with glass, about burying the bar's owner in a shallow grave while he suffocated on worms and dirt.

Before the drama, Luna used to come into Rex's with her husband, a tall, gorgeous man with dark skin and long eyelashes. He was a decent guy but was never right for her. I served them both plenty of times (always a foaming beer for him and a whiskey sour for her), but never spoke to Luna much until after the bottle incident. Rex's was too busy for small talk with patrons.

We became fast friends. My ache for her was instant. She was the night come to life, a dewdrop of shimmering darkness wearing a bubblegum pink dress and identical heels.

We went out alone one night to a bar she'd never been to, and the intoxication of her flowery perfume and vodka-stained lips was suddenly too near and too far away. My mouth found hers. She kissed back hard and needy, only to pull away with ruined lipstick and wide eyes.

"Shit, Andi." Her glance darted away, but smooth fingers intertwined with mine. "I've never cheated on my husband with a woman before. Okay, that came out wrong. I've never cheated on him with *anyone*. You know what I mean."

I did. She jumped away and disappeared into a taxi.

And then she came to my house the next night.

She and Malik were on the rocks before I came along. The divorce paperwork had already been in a slow process for their disintegrating marriage. At least that's what I like to tell myself.

When it was finalized, she stumbled into my house with a look of both relief and sadness.

"Do you regret the divorce?"

She shook her head. "Malik isn't a bad man, you know? We got married young, and we grew apart. He wants kids and a momma to stay home and watch those kids. I don't want anything to do with that."

I smiled at her, already hopelessly in love. "Me neither. I just want you."

"Plus," she said, "I think my interest in romantic partners is uhm, a little different than when I was a teenager." The warmth of her hand on my upper thigh sent a thousand tiny bolts of electricity through my flesh.

"Would you ever want to be with him again, if he changed his mind about the future?"

She laughed out a musical melody and my heart sang along.

"No way. We're going to try and be friends, but I don't love him romantically." Her eyes shone as she looked into mine.

Malik had called me once, drunk and heartbroken, which is the only reason I ever forgave the things he said. What he shouted at me wasn't anything new, the same furious slurs I'd heard my whole life, but when he bitched out Luna and threatened my girl, I let him know I'd gouge his eyes out with fishhooks if he hurt her.

I don't think he ever would. He loves her too much, but he had the wrath that night and I understood him. Maybe that was the worst part, how you can understand a stranger because you know their pain, because you helped cause their pain.

———•———

When I pull up the road, it's nearly noon and the vultures are resting in three of the big trees that dot the property line. I try to ignore them and look away but can't stop daydreaming about growing wings and flying with the flock. A family.

A family who eats carrion. Laughter bubbles free and true for the first time today. Part of me feels like they've been watching during the entire session, as if they followed on invisible wings and eavesdropped as intently as Dr. Fawning seemed to listen.

A cherry red Ford parked at the house rocks gently in the breeze. My mind calms, picturing Luna's dark curls tangling in the wind, the car's windows rolled down in the summer, her singing along to the radio.

The gravel and dried mud crunch beneath bootsteps. The sun lends its warmth, but the wind chill is less forgiving. As soon as I open the door and spot Luna lounging on the living room couch, the chill dissipates. The midnight of her eyes instantly focuses on me. In her focus, I find my center and sanity.

"Hey Andi." She smiles and sits up, patting the space on the couch next to her. "How was it?"

I flop down and rest my head on her shoulder, already eager to forget this morning's humiliation. She tangles smooth fingers through the auburn strands of my hair, sending waves of comfort and love with every stroke. We share so many interests, our passions for woodsy walks and driving around to every park in the state, taking silly photos and dreaming of traveling away. But our differences really drew me to her.

Where I was pale and timid and dressed from head-to-toe in black, Luna glowed like the center of a Brown-Eyed-Susan—she was outgoing, wicked smart, and wore striking, patterned scarves and long, colorful dresses that contrasted beautifully against her skin. The moon to my sun, keeping me balanced in a world where my own brain wages civil war with emotions.

"Hello," Luna says and flutters a smooth hand with two shiny, emerald rings in front of me. I bring her fingers to my cheek.

"Earth to Andi."

"Hmm?"

"How's the new chick?" Luna tilts her head and raises a perfectly arched eyebrow. The faint, lime-green of her eyeshadow glitters above the long lashes.

"Quiet. I did most of the talking. Her suit was funny."

"Funny how?"

"Well who wears an all-tan suit? It looked weird."

Luna laughs and each note of it is like a delicate wind chime singing the most beloved of songs. "I guess if that's your only complaint, then she must be okay." She eyes my black leggings and oversized black sweater covered in hair and lint. "The suit is probably fine, too. Like you're some fashionista." She rolls her eyes in pretend mockery, and we tackle each other into the corner of the couch.

She sighs against my ear and clicks her tongue to the roof of her mouth, which means she was going to say something but changed her mind.

"What is it?" I pull away and stare her down.

"Nothing."

"Come on, Luna. Don't make me beg," I say and then wink. She laughs a little and sighs again.

"It's stupid, really. I know you need to deal with things in your own way. It's just…ugh. You're going to hate me! Especially after this morning. I'm really sorry again."

"I could never hate you." My hands grip her hands. "Please tell me."

"It's like I feel left out or something. Maybe that's not the right term. Maybe I'm jealous, which is insane because it's not like I want to make you open up and tell me all these morbid details, but there's this whole part of you and your life story you've told therapists but not me. Am I fucked up to think that? Is it even fair for me to ask this?"

"You're always allowed to ask me anything, Luna-bug."

She beams at the silly nickname. A sharp inhale fights its way into my lungs.

"Well, you know most of it."

My body fidgets around on the couch and I shift away. Her patient eyes shine but she doesn't reach out, perhaps sensing my need for space.

"My little brother died when he was four, you know that part," I say, and she nods, her lips pulled in tight. "He climbed out to the roof and fell onto the cement patio. My father was crushed, guilt-ridden, and crazy. My mom tried to be strong, but the demons in her mind pulverized her, begged her to give up, but she didn't. She survived, for me. I never realized how close my father had been to snapping. He spared me because I was at a sleepover that night, too far away of a target for his temporary but fatal breakdown."

My fingers curl into a fist, absentmindedly beating a bruising rhythm against my thigh until Luna's warm hand holds it still. Heartbeats pound in my ear with a loud, steady cadence.

"He tied my mom up in his old truck with the already cracked windshield. Drove them both into the freezing Schuylkill River. The police told me she almost survived the water. The drugs in her system didn't subdue her for too long, but somewhere between the crash and the truck sinking, broken shards of ice from the river poured in through the crushed windshield and pierced her eyes." The words waterfall out, rushing to exorcise their raw pain before courage falters.

"After they died, no one wanted to be around me. I was a mean, morbid girl, and I resented everyone and their perfect, *living* family members. Every day at school was a challenge, a dare for someone to piss off the angry chick with the dead family."

No one understood or cared to try and understand. They had no idea what it was like seeing my mother hauled from the lake. The way water and other fluids leaked from her mouth and ears and nose, her crystal blue eyes nothing more than gored, sinewy sockets of emptiness.

Luna winces and slowly untangles her hand from mine. My fingernails had dug deep crescents into her skin. My mouth opens to offer an apology, but a smothered sob breaks free instead. Her arms wrap around my shaking body. Hot tears stream down and into my mouth, leaving behind salty apologies in the after-silence.

—•—

Even with Luna's warm arms wrapped around me, the vultures still visit my dreams. My beautiful partner with her wind chime laugh cannot keep them away. The birds are there, nestled inside my mind's tombstone labyrinth, and they stare at me from atop my families' gravestones.

3:00am glowers red numbers from the clock on the nightstand. I am desperately trying to recapture those misted, scattered dream-thoughts into the net of my conscious memories. My old therapist was there, muttering from a hospital bed cushioned between naked trees. I couldn't understand her, but the vultures did. They circled and listened, a tornado of wings and beaks awaiting her command.

Vultures are relatively quiet creatures, but in my dream, they wouldn't stop hissing until my dead therapist sliced her arm open. Cancer revealed itself as a murky, black clog of bile, seeping from her forearm and pooling onto the forest soil.

Hissing turned to screaming and the buzzards dove furiously around my head, demanding I taste her cancer.

The curdled chunks of the disease were so appalling it woke me up. And as I lie on the sweat-soaked sheets straining to capture my breath, trying not to violently twitch away and wake Luna, the fuzzy aftertaste of vinegary sludge lingers on in the back of my throat.

Thirst becomes a desperate need, and I slip away from Luna's clutch and walk into the kitchen. Cool water offers a small reprieve from the imaginary taste but does nothing to keep the vultures out of my head.

What does it taste like—dead flesh? Do the bodies haunt the vultures after they consume the carcass? If I eat a human's meat, do they live on inside me forever? Humans eat cooked ham, steak, venison, and more all the time. All those dead cows, chickens, pigs, fish—they become meals. Their bodies digesting inside another body. Bones and organs, blood and marrow, absorbing and taking what each part needs to survive. It's cooked, preserved, safe.

Everything is always so safe here. Savory and sheltered.

My mind wades back into the Schuylkill River's water. Before I knew my parents were gone, I came home from the rocky sleepover in the morning and was hoping to be greeted by the aroma of my mother's breakfast creations, usually scrambled eggs with cheese and the cherry tomatoes from our garden. Only old chimney smoke from the fire we made two nights before lingered in the air. Wind gusts had traveled down and stirred up the charred logs.

It would be two more days until they found my parents in the river, until I saw my mother's shattered face and ruined eyes. What if I had saved part of her skin or brain or liquids before she was buried? Maybe she'd be living inside me, a small part of her, whispering and guiding me through this life. My whole family, they could be here suspended within my body rather than remembered as skeletons buried inside my bone-castle of memories.

Maybe I could have kept them forever. Is this what the vultures do? These guardians of the underworld, these eaters of flesh and souls, what are the secrets hidden inside their curving vertebrae?

The longing to hold something dead against my tongue consumes me like a starvation. The power of it floods my body stronger than the sin of wrath ever has. Can dead flesh hold anger?

Mine would. Mine would be the most excruciatingly bitter of them all.

"Andi?"

Luna's sleepy call echoes down the hallway. Should I tell her these thoughts, how they scatter around in my brain like thrown marbles? She'd probably crease her brow at me, try to make sense of my newest obsession through a half-awake state of mind.

Images of her repulsion toward the moth wings leaks into my brain like an uninvited rain storm. She has no idea how hard I have to fight myself to keep the anger away.

So no, for now, this is mine. My secret. My need to know and understand the vultures.

3

ello?? Seriously, Andi?

Luna's annoyed text message lights up the phone screen. For whatever reason, my mind has entrapped itself in a dark place this week, the kind of darkness where it's better to avoid the people you love.

This happened before, me disappearing and ignoring everyone. Most people stopped caring about trying to find me, except Luna. One time she tracked me to the rooftop of an old, abandoned convenience store downtown. I rambled about my brother and how I had to save him from the fall. Climbing up to the rooftop was a memory I never recovered. I remembered muttering my brother's name over and over. It was like a blackout from too much booze, but I rarely drink, even when I worked at Rex's.

I didn't trust myself enough to drink, to smoke, to do anything involved with letting my guard down because wrath would emerge again. Worse than ever. Needing to slice someone open like that man from the bar.

Luna's last voice message goes through a range of emotions. She stopped by the house, but I was out, picking up some dinner. My heart demands, *call her,* but my brain knows better. She shouldn't be around me right now, even if it seems cruel to ignore her. If I called back and said it was for her own good to leave me be for a bit, it would ignite a war with the only person I love. Her temporary anger and permanent safety are the better options.

The rotisserie chicken dinner tempts my mind back into the kitchen. My stomach growls in want as I remove the blue plastic bag and free the cooked bird from its plastic prison. Condensation drips from the still warm lid, and the liquid reminds me of Dr. Fawning's dewy eyes today when she'd said my love for Luna is more obsession than real love.

The plastic lid crunches from my hands twisting it up. If I was obsessed with Luna, I wouldn't ignore her all week with the intention of protecting her. I'd be creeping outside her apartment with a camera, watching her through the windows or some perverted shit. Or sending her dead moth wings in the mail.

Dr. Fawning said I will figure that out in time, but I don't understand what she means. I don't dislike the doctor, necessarily, but she's so quiet and abstract with her whispers and stares. I need guidance to fill the empty ache in my body. Otherwise, I am forever starving for help, unsure of how to ask for it.

My stomach gurgles again and I eye the body of meat wrapped around the chicken's skeleton. A tempting and warm aroma of roasted skin and seasoning perfume together. It smells good, but something is missing.

I pick off a strip of tender chicken breast. I am eating with the vultures. This chicken, my roadkill. My eyes close. The chicken grows a head and feathers. Coyotes come to tear the body open. Instead of lips, my mouth morphs to a beak and I gnaw along its carcass.

Deceased and moist. My jaws work the meat into pulps, and in my imagination my own feathers shiver in the glorious feeling of an anticipated feast. The juice slathers my lips like a greasy gloss as I dive deeper into the container.

How different would it really taste as something raw and untouched?

Disgust never works its way into my reactions, only curiosity. Carrion *has* to be repulsive and inedible to a human, otherwise why would our ancestors have built fires to roast their fresh kills? But how do I know these things for sure? If Dr. Fawning won't give me the guidance I seek to live a life free from the torment inside my vicious thoughts, then maybe the vultures will.

They have been here since the days of the Old World, constantly evolving, scattering around the continents and adapting. And they will be here long after the rest of us are gone. Their beaks will make a banquet of our decay. Our deaths deserve no other meaning than to be devoured. Our bodies have ruined the earth, it seems only right such bodies should give back to nature, to the animals. Because then it does not matter if society declares your face or skin or features wrong, we are all bodies waiting to be swallowed into soil, into the ocean.

When my eyes close, I am standing next to them. My body hunched down with rippling black and brown feathers shining in the sun as I stretch the muscles and tendons of my new wings. I join the vultures in their wake, magnificent figures circling a dead beast as if in ritual for what is to take place.

My teeth gnaw at the meat around a bone from the rotisserie chicken. This isn't enough. Isn't raw enough. Even if I went to a restaurant and ordered a bloody steak, it wouldn't be right. They'd still cook it into safety because again, everything is so safe here. Preserved and burnt.

I could purchase raw meat at the grocery store, but it wouldn't be the same. I need to *know* what the vultures know, and they sure as hell aren't walking into stores and carrying out plastic bags of packaged flanks and tenderloins.

None of this is enough. I shove the cooked chicken away and listen to my stomach conducting its petulant orchestra. Even when

I tried to explain the cravings to Dr. Fawning, she stared back with those big eyes and remained quiet. What exactly am I paying this woman for, again?

The questions simmer in my brain, fueling rage like volcanic bile through my chest. Wrath waits in this purgatory of hunger and anger. The really bad kind that consumes me whole, blacks out portions of my day.

The only thing Dr. Fawning did say earlier was some bullshit metaphor about raw meat representing a desire for sex and blah blah blah, heard it all before.

Or maybe I told myself this. I don't remember.

I'm just so fucking hungry.

The need to escape these festering and harmful thoughts leads me to venture outside for a brief winter walk. The slap of cold air against my face starts to reset my mind. Sharp bursts of arctic atmosphere billow down into the recesses of my throat and lungs. Across the road, the sunset casts dying sherbet tones of light. Dirt and dead leaves punch a cold, earthy scent through the wind gusts.

Mr. Landon is guiding a giant pig away from his truck's hauler and toward the barn. He looks up as I approach and I give him a wave. The old farmer is bundled in blue plaid flannel and his eyes blink at me from behind oversized glasses.

"Pretty, ain't she?" He gestures toward the pig as she retreats into the barn with her swinging belly. The curled tail wiggles a bit and she grunts as we stand in the door and watch her settle into a corner of cloth and hay.

"Poor girl got pregnant at the wrong time and then her owner didn't want her. The idiot should have kept her isolated from the males then. They can't afford the feed right now, so I'm taking her in. She's ready to give birth any day now." Mr. Landon talks about the pig like a proud father, but no sympathy stirs within me. Only the return of a stabbing famine.

"How many will she have?"

"Might be about six or eight in her litter, might be more. Hard to tell until it's happening."

The mother emits a series of grunts and Mr. Landon steps into the barn to check on her and place a hand on her swollen body. She seems friendly and noses at him the way a happy dog would. Her nest of straw is thick and surrounded by a three-sided structure of plywood. Fresh water waits in a big bowl nearby, catching the silver reflection of what's behind her.

Up on the wall rests a layout of different tools. A mud-caked shovel, one rusted rake, and a few spades, shears, and axes.

The shears look sharp enough to cut into the mother pig's belly, to slice through the pink skin and teats. Her stomach could pop like a water balloon full of hidden blood and babies. The way her insides would spill into a crimson pool across the straw, and the piglets swimming their way out of their mother's warmth and toward me—still alive and squealing. It'd be so easy to take one or two. Grab the axe and sever the umbilical cords. One piglet for the vultures to show me how it's done. One for me to try, to taste, to swallow down and satisfy the ache in my abdomen.

Mr. Landon says something, but I turn away and run from the barn back toward my house. Tears sting in the corners of my eyes as the wind chill hits. I do my best to squash down the twinging inside me, the awakened craving for raw meat.

The sharp, watchful gaze of the vultures pierces through the night, the woods, the field, all the way into my house. Even when I close the door and all the blinds, their vigilant curiosity follows.

—•—

"Come over," I say to Luna in the morning. Her voice on the other end of the phone is barely awake. It's been too long, and I need her badly, need her to make me human again.

"You're okay?"

"Sort of." My free hand pulls at a white thread on the comforter.

"Enough for me to be mad at you?"

"Yes."

"Good," she says and pauses. Static clicks across the line.

"I'm really sorry."

When she arrives, I apologize once more, but the hunger refuses to stop storming inside my gut. Maybe being close to someone will help ease the thunder. An ache fills my brain to trace fingertips along her smooth sides, her neck, her arms...

My body buzzes toward her like a moth to a beautiful sunbeam.

"I want you," I say before she even has her coat off. She stops midway through unzipping it, and I almost hate the begging in my own voice. But I need the solace of her touch, her kiss, her moans in my ears.

She sighs and squirms away from my reaching hands. "I can't right now, Andi. You know…"

I know, but I don't care. Never have. She's always the one to put off sex until her period finishes or tell me she'll make it up to me when mine is over.

"Are you really so squeamish about some blood?" I tease her and then kiss the dark pout of her lips. She doesn't push me away. The yearning to crawl inside the warmth of her washes over me like the steamed heat of an opened oven door. For her, I would disintegrate inside steam. For her, I would burn.

She breaks away from my hungry mouth. "Oh fuck that, and fuck whoever decided women were squeamish of blood in the first place."

I hold my hands up in surrender. "I didn't say women were. Just *you*."

"I am not!" she cries out, giving me a defensive glare. "Periods and babies and women who work as nurses and doctors, all this shit and someone out there decided women can't handle blood."

I roll my eyes, spurring her on. "I know, but hey, it's fine. My tough Luna, scared of her own blood."

She crosses her arms, but I know the glint in her eyes. I know what hunger looks like.

"Then let me touch you, if you really aren't afraid." I kiss her hard and she leans into my arms before pulling back.

"But it's, I mean, it's a little weird, right?"

My hand squeezes hers. "No one's judging us, Luna-bug, it's only me and you here. I've missed you so much." The tip of my nose touches hers and we breathe in the same, heated air.

"Then why did you ignore me all week?" she whispers.

"Because I'm an idiot."

She laughs her wind chime laugh and the world becomes right again.

"Please, let me make you feel good." I nuzzle into her neck, inhale the flowered perfume.

She pulls back and narrows her eyes. "Damn you. Give me a second." She disappears into the bathroom for a moment, but when she returns she kisses me hard this time. My body leads hers to the bedroom and her fists ball up the sweater I'm wearing as we fall onto the bed. I trail a ribbon of kisses down her sighing body, snaking my tongue along her abdomen and darkening her belly. My fingers shake as I unbutton her jeans, tremble from all this holding back I had to do since she walked in the door. The slow slide of her pants and soft, black panties over the curves of her hips lights a twisted fire through my chest. When I'm nestled between her warm thighs and skating my fingers closer, she reaches a hand down and places it on my wrist.

"Andi, you don't have to do this," she says, her eyes giving way to the nervousness bubbling inside.

"Shush," I reply and move up to kiss her neck, her soft chest. My hands unable to stop roaming the silken plains of her long body.

Luna's fingers tangle in my hair as my lips whisper around her nipples and down against her ribs. Goosebumps ripple across the dark skin and I lick them away. "I owe you some pleasure for my being an absent bitch this week."

She laughs a little and I move down to kiss her thighs again, letting fingertips run along the inner velvet warmth as her legs pry wider apart. When I slide a finger into her wetness, she stutters out a moan, as if she wanted to try and stop me again but changed her mind. My head descends to take her into my mouth, careful to keep my lips where she wants me and not where will make her more nervous. It's only a little blood. The raw liquid of my gorgeous girl, flowing through her vessel and keeping her warm and alive.

My tongue conducts a melody against her sensitive center, and every moan and sigh sing along to the song we create together. I glance up and watch the sweet rise and fall of her chest, the way her full lips part and how she sometimes takes her lower lip between her teeth. My tongue continues to trace patterns of musical notes against her. I hum and she groans, burying her fingers deeper into my loose hair.

The concentrated expression on her face is such a beautiful sight as I slide in a second finger and she grinds against me. She is lost in a simple, electric pleasure, and the knowledge of how lost she is almost makes me not do it, but the tang of metallic blood on my fingers strengthens right below where my nose is buried in her soft flesh.

I work her harder, curving my fingers along her ridges, sliding against the spots that make her moan the loudest. Everything is so slick and hot inside her. More blood smears on my fingers. Burning, red need stains my vision.

My stomach rumbles a command and I have to know, have to

understand what power blood holds. Does the blood of the dead taste different? I may never know, but the blood of the living, maybe it's the closest I'll ever get to understanding the vultures and tasting what they taste. Knowing what they know.

Luna moans loud and her body's vibrations quake against my lips. My mouth reluctantly moves away. Her eyes flutter open, and I imagine what I must look like, kneeling between her legs with my hair mussed and my eyes wild in hunger, with her period blood coated on my fingers from tip to past the knuckles. She exhales something I don't quite hear as I slip each finger into my mouth, let the blood soak on my tongue. My lips suck flesh and nail until it's all gone, both the bright, smooth smears and the thicker clots from the lining shedding away inside her.

All of it.

The metallic bitterness curls my tongue away at first as I get used to the taste. The coppery tang turns exotic and sweet as I run a finger against my teeth, enjoying the sensation and wanting more. I inhale against my hand and breathe the blood in deep. Eyes open, I bend down to collect more, nudging my head between her trembling thighs.

Luna thrusts her hand out and her palm smacks against my forehead, stopping me. Her knees snap together before she springs up and off the bed. She stares, mouth open and distorted in an emotion I don't want to name because she looks so distraught. Instant loathing brews within me because I am the one who brought such horror to her face, to the person I was supposed to be making up my shitty disappearance to.

"What the fuck, Andi?" She jumps off the bed and grabs her pants and underwear from the floor. The bathroom door slams shut as I stay kneeling in the bed, the sticky mess of my fingers and the ache in my gut and on my tongue all here with me, present ghosts asking me yeah, what the fuck am I doing? And also asking, *oh god, why did you stop? Why did you let her go?*

The hunger worsens, but my heart is racing. I lick a little more at my knuckles and for one fucked up second, I imagine Luna dead and splayed open, her blood and meat all still and tender for me to taste and touch and have as my own as I circle above her, hissing at the other vultures because she is mine and mine alone. Her body a shiny, earthen beacon with the forest's foliage spreading beneath her like the lime wings of the Luna moths. Like her eyeshadow and emerald rings. I could consume her and keep her in me forever.

My palm *whaps* hard against my cheek, slapping the image from my head. *Stop, you idiot, stop.*

I stumble over to the bathroom. There are stifled cries coming from the other side of the door and my heart shatters.

"Luna, I'm so sorry." My forehead presses against the cool wood of the door.

"Go away. I don't want to talk to you."

"Hey, you said it yourself, women aren't queasy because of some blood. All we seem to do is bleed and—"

"That's a lot different than sucking up someone's menstrual blood like a goddamn perverted vampire!"

I'd laugh if she didn't sound so disgusted.

"I'm really sorry," I say instead.

The bathroom door whooshes open and I stumble forward. Luna pushes her way past, fully dressed and her mouth set in a hard line. She grabs her coat from the living room couch. She goes to slip her boots back on too and I know I'm in trouble now. She never just leaves. We always talk through our problems and always have, ever since everything with Malik. Even during the times I disappeared, we always talked about it more afterward.

"Please don't go," I whisper. A deep swirling ache of sadness and famine funnel together inside my stomach. Maybe I should let her go, but I'm greedy and obscene and I don't want her to leave.

She turns around but keeps a hand on the doorknob. "I love you, Andi, but you're freaking me out. Get yourself straight, and then call me." Those beautiful, dark eyes blink once, and then she's gone.

If only the hunger could leave so quickly, too. My steps guide me into the bathroom and to the sink. Warm tap water and soap soak my hands, but the remaining scarlet stains prove stubborn in their removal. Scalding water morphs pale hands into a sore pink.

When my skin is scrubbed raw, I turn the faucet off and dry my hands on the black towel above the small garbage bin. Water drips down and bounces off the plastic bag in the bin. A balled-up roll of toilet paper rests in the bottom next to a lone string of floss. Saliva fills my mouth as I hunch down and thrust my hand into the trash.

"Oh god." My words whisper to an empty space. A hard lump forms behind my tongue. The toilet paper wad unrolls in my hands like unwrapping a present. A secret gift from Luna.

Her bloody tampon sticks to the paper, but it's still damp and warm from its time inside her wonderful body. My hands shake as I hold the cotton up to my nose and inhale. Heat spreads low in my abdomen and I squirm from my seat on the closed toilet lid. One hand slips beneath the stretchy band of my leggings, gliding into the wet warmth between my legs. My other hand holds the tampon to my lips and my tongue darts out to taste what Luna left behind.

4

"When the stars threw down their spears

And water'd heaven with their tears:

Did he smile his work to see?

Did he who made the Lamb make thee?"

—William Blake, "The Tyger"

The oblivion of sleep turns to nightmares. Luna's taste still dances on my tongue, even in the altered consciousness of terrible dreams. Feral hunger slinks through the groan of my bones when I wake up and stretch. 7:23pm. Winter's darkness consumes the world outside, except for a twinkle of light from Mr. Landon's house across the field. Another light shines from the barn where the pig rests. Did she have her babies yet?

There's a missed call from Luna and a voicemail on my phone. The want to call her back lingers, but my stomach rumbles a series of cramp-worthy gurgles.

How her blood weighed on my tongue, turning iron to honey. My Luna.

Numbing wind-chill tears through my thin sweater and the frozen dirt spikes against my bare toes. A tango of shivers command I retreat back into my house, but I've already walked this far. Might as well check and see.

My appetite grows sentient with every step toward the barn, demanding I, who am nothing more than a ravenous body in the night, continue my search for a meal. I am a beast with an urge and I must placate it. This is what animals do.

There's a dying calf outside the barn in a nest of straw. If it's already dying from whatever made the others sick earlier this winter, then maybe I shouldn't…if the animal was sick, would its meat make me sick, too? The calf is skinny and its face droops. The vultures will have him soon enough.

I wander closer, past cows and chicken coops, taking care not to tramp my bare feet into any piles of animal shit. The barn door is closed but unlocked, so it slides open easily with a quick squeak. A muted, warming light casts elongated shadows over the barn's brown walls. Mr. Landon's only horse gives a soft whinny from her stall and watches with black, blinking eyes. Her chestnut mane is shiny and long. She's a beautiful creature.

In the far-left corner, the sow rests while her newborn piglets suckle and sleep. She doesn't take her eyes off me, just watches as I shuffle closer. Maybe she remembers me from yesterday. I kneel and let her sniff my hand like I would with a cat. She grunts a bit and seems to accept me as nonthreatening. Her eyes express a drowsy intelligence and I coo softly at the new mother as she fades into sleep.

"There now, what a brave girl you are. What a good mother."

The piglets are so small and surprisingly not as ugly as many other newborn animals. The tiny tails and ears wriggle as the babies stay attached to their mother. Mr. Landon must have cleaned up well because there isn't much blood or signs of birth in the bedding.

Only the mulchy odor of hay and tired animals circulates around the barn.

Seven pink snouts nose around at the sow's big belly, and I slowly reach a hand to caress one piglet's back as it drifts into sleep. The tiny body is warm and lax, thrumming with new life. The mother fidgets but doesn't squeal or bite. I hum a little to them, mother and piglets, willing a deep sleep to take hold of all as my lullaby continues.

The rumbling in my stomach turns to pinching cramps, threatening to seize up and shred my insides like cat claws against fraying ribbons. I close my eyes and try to will the pain away. Instead, I see the vultures circling like they did that first morning in the periwinkle sky. They hiss at me, spitting into my head in angry wonder, mocking me for my weakness. How long will it take me to prove myself, to show them my carrion prey?

Axes and shears along the wall greet me when my eyes open back up. Their blades glint in the shadows, reflecting the barn's light. My hands are reaching, searching, slowly wrapping beneath the tiny creature's soft, warm belly and snatching it away from its mother.

One hand clamps tight over the piglet's snout to keep it quiet. The mother doesn't squeal until I'm already halfway out of the barn door and she finally opens up those sleepy eyes. Her squeal is more scream than anything else, but she also sounds so tired. So broken. Momma had a hard day, but so did I. The hay pokes at my feet, and I trip over a loose pile of bricks outside the barn. Scraping pain from the rough surface stings against my toes, but I keep racing toward the trees to disappear into darkness's cover.

Mr. Landon's porch door swings shut with a hard rattle in its frame.

"Who's out here?" he bellows across the yard.

The piglet wriggles with feisty gusto for such a small thing. Its little hooves dig painfully into my ribs as I press it close against my body, quieting the creature. My fingers stroke down the soft back.

"There now, hush."

Grumbles from the old man echo closer. He stops by the open barn door and disappears inside. Frantic heartbeats pound in my head as I bolt away, into the black night. I carefully traipse deeper into the thin woods and keep my clutch over the piglet's mouth tight until its frightful shrieks are snuffed out. There is a slight clearing among the trees, a familiar copse I've sat in before.

Acidic appetite burns all other thoughts away. The growling in my abdomen jells from hunger and anticipation, begging me to feed it and give the caustic slosh roiling inside something to digest. Do the vultures see? Are they circling now in the night and watching, judging my character and this test of strength? If I *can* understand them, maybe they will accept me like a long-lost progeny. Maybe I am something bigger than myself, a descendant of virulent animals who feast on the dead.

The piglet's shrieks break through my loose hand and the creature won't shut up. My grip tightens over the snout, clamping everything together nice and tight while I think...*tighter*, and I think, tighter, tighter, *Jesus Christ* grant me silence you squealing brat. Squeeze the snout and, oh *fucking hell*. Warm liquid spurts onto my hands and drips down, staining my boots. Throttle the neck. Something snaps, and the night is so quiet, leaving the reek of piss to deal with. The baby in my arms turns to dead weight.

I add another gravestone to the cemetery in my mind.

"Ugh." I try to fling some of the piss off my jacket, but it doesn't help.

I have nothing to bury you with. Nothing to slice you open. I should have taken those damned shears after all, but then it'd look more likely a human had done this. Maybe the old farmer will think a coyote or raccoon snatched the piglet.

There is little moonlight tonight and I can barely see the pale, pink body hanging limp from my hands. Tiny and soft…still warm.

The vultures had their beaks. I have my teeth.

My stomach howls so loudly I think Mr. Landon will surely hear it. I am twitching, starving. Pissed Luna walked out on me. Heartbroken by the heavy graveyard weighing inside my head.

The black sky turns red. With a forward lurch, I bury my face into the piglet's body, rubbing its fuzzy rind against my lips and cheeks. My teeth chomp hard along the skin. A pointed ear grazes my lips and I grind off the tip before ripping out a bigger chunk. Blood splatters past my lips, soaking the gums and slicking my molars with surprising sweetness. Teeth and nails work together to spread open the cheek and jowls, filling my mouth with young meat. My thumbnail slips and sticks in the piglet's eye, and I lap up the thin, tart liquid I find there. My throat tightens, gags, not from the metallic, grassy taste but from how much is stuffed into my jaws. Desperation drives me to frenzy; to shred the piglet's flesh and discover what waits hidden inside, what tempts the vultures to carry bits of the dead within their own bodies.

I chew and chew at what gurgles out of the spread open body, wishing my incisors and canines were all razor-sharp fangs. A piranha mouth to devour my sinewy prize.

Everything cools quickly in the winter night, but still I bury my face in deep and sample juices and organs, biting around the rib bones, but the bones are so small. Bite and taste and slurp until I can't see, until my gut sends a signal up to my brain saying, *satisfied, please stop for tonight.* There is nothing left of the piglet I can masticate any further.

Overhead, I pray the vultures watch. Pray they understand me now as I am finally understanding them.

—•—

"Get up." Luna's voice cuts through the fog of sleep. My eyes fight through morning crust and finally open. Her figure blurs into vision, and she looms with crossed arms above me. The faded blue walls of the living room come into focus. A groaning twinge cracks through my back from sleeping on the couch.

My hands are clean. My clothes, too. A vague memory of showering after coming home last night rolls in my brain like mist. How stained my mouth and face were…blood and then dirt from where I buried the piglet's remains.

"Nice to see you, too," I grumble and sit up, clutching my stomach.

Her glare could cut through glass. Today her midnight curls are pushed back with a dark, red headscarf. Her V-neck sweater matches perfectly. The crimson against her flesh reminds me how sweetly her blood had honeyed against my taste buds.

"You haven't been going to your sessions," she says.

"What are you talking about?" I try to make sense of her words through my morning grog, but the sudden memory of what I did last night rushes over me in nauseous waves like a hangover hammering inside my brain.

"Mr. Landon flagged me down this morning," she continues. "When I was driving up to make sure you weren't dead since you can't return phone calls, apparently."

I hear the snort push out of my nose before I can stop it. "Because you really wanted to talk to me, right?"

"Yeah, I did."

I grind my teeth in an effort to reduce all the stupid things I want to say. "And what about Landon? One, he's super weird. Two, he isn't part of my therapy so how the hell would he know if I go or not?" I get up and push past her, suddenly desperate to make it to the toilet.

"You always liked him well enough before. I mean, he's been your neighbor forever."

"He's crazy," I say in a half-choked whisper because I am definitely going to vomit.

"He sounded pretty sane to me. Andi, stop." She grabs at my wrist. "He said you've been parking your car in the woods along the pull off on his property like you're trying to hide it. And then he said you walk off into the trees every Monday morning, for hours."

"And why would I do that?" I do my best to keep my tone even, but there it is…rippling inside me. Bitterness. Wrath. The roiling rage of it threatens to overpour and spill out of my throat.

Or maybe it's the dead pig rooting in my intestines. "I have not been walking into the fucking woods. I have been seeing Dr. Fawning. Now get out of my way before I puke on you."

I rush into the bathroom and barely make it to the toilet bowl. My unwashed hair sweeps down as I grab the cool porcelain of the commode to keep balanced.

"Are you sick?" Luna's voice is more concern than anger now.

I open my mouth to answer, but my body jolts forward. My stomach turns inside out and something horribly sour and painful tears up through my esophagus. Tiny shrapnel-like pieces cut along my throat as warm vomit chokes me before spilling out into the toilet. The smell hits me first and is worse than any flu bug or other puking I've ever experienced.

My eyes are watering so much I can barely see as a second wave announces its presence and splits through, forcing my mouth open for it to roil out in a sick perversion of a waterfall. Deep red mixes in with thick, yellow bile. Tears sting at my eyes, mutating the world into a blur as I gasp to catch my breath from the heaving. Rancid burning stings my throat, as if I swallowed razors. My hands twitch against the toilet bowl in movements I cannot control, jerking in reaction to the pain inside my neck.

There are soft footsteps behind me as Luna comes to hold my hair away from my dripping mouth. Her hands rub my back as she clutches the strands in a ponytail. She tightens her grip and puffs out a breath.

"Are those…bones?"

I blink away the tears and wipe them off with a tissue Luna hands me. I finally stare into the toilet. Mixed in with chunks of gooey, barely-digested meat and watery blood are small bones I must have somehow swallowed from last night. I peer closer and swear I see even tinier, clipped down teeth.

My stomach burbles, but all I hear are the squeals of a baby piglet.

"What the fuck, Andi?"

I spit the remnants of sour bile into the toilet. "They must have been in the chicken I got from the store last night. Didn't even notice." My voice is raspy and unconvincing, but Luna pulls my face away from the toilet and flushes it all down for me. She strokes my back for five minutes as I dry-heave before a third and final wave of acerbic vomit demands to be exorcised from my body. I gag it out in retching bursts until my stomach has no more to give.

Emptiness harbors a grudge inside my belly, resenting me for feeding it what I hungered for. I have been betrayed by my body. Dead meat I worked to steal and carry away like a bandit coyote in the night has spewed out from the dark grottos inside me. The secrets I locked down in the cellar of my gut have crawled away to expose their horrors into the light. My mind cruelly sends me an image of the mother pig, bereft and knowing her baby is gone. All for nothing. My sustenance, all my justifications, they have been expelled from my body without my approval.

Is this a lesson? The vultures, they have to be teaching me something from this. Have to be…

Luna pulls me away and flushes it all down again, not asking any more questions. Somewhere in my despair and haze, she undresses us both and shoves me into the shower. Her body is comforting and warm next to mine, and part of me wants to curl into her and sob as the water cascades again

to try and explain what I have done. I sta

letting her fix me, as always.

After the shower, she feeds me Listerii

purging the terrible aftertaste of stomach ac

a black robe hanging from the bathroom dooi

own clothes again. By the time we walk into   _ oit

across from each other on the bed, I feel more _..c a human. The

gray blankets beckon to curl beneath them and sleep, but Luna is

on edge, picking at a stray thread on the comforter. She wants to

tell me how she really feels, but she's scared. I can see that. I used to

know everything about her movements, her quirks, her kinks, every

twitch of her expressive face, all those gestures and micro expres-

sions were my poetry every day, my Bible I read from; her—the only

one I could ever pray to and trust. And I have smashed all of our

love down into unrepairable pieces. My girl with nighttime skin and

eyes full of starry constellations, what have I done to you?

I have pushed everything good away because of this deep need

in me to understand the vultures. To build my wings and earn a

freedom of my own. I could never be anything more than a copy of

them, but I still want it because it feels like *mine*.

They have a secret. I still have so much more to understand.

"Andi, I don't know where to start." Luna's damp hair tangles

her curls tightly together. She crosses her arms and the crimson

sweater tightens around her chest. She is so sad and so beautiful,

and I hate myself for equating the two things together.

"Then don't. Lie down here with me."

"I want to…" She doesn't look at me. "But why haven't you

been going to your sessions? I know how important it is for you to

talk to someone after everything."

"I have been!" My legs wobble when I stand up. "I fucking have

been, every Monday morning. I get in my car, I drive down the road, awning, and that woman, she just stares at me! She think, but she doesn't talk. She stares with those big, dark s and her sandy hair, and those goddamn tan-colored suits look like some sad animal's skin. It's always the same."

"Mr. Landon said—"

"If you're going to believe the old bastard over me then get out, Luna. Just go away."

"Andi…"

"I mean it!" I hover in front of her, anger consuming my every nerve. "If this is how you want to be after everything, then leave."

The molten pain of pure hurt simmers in her eyes, and the last thing I really want her to do is leave, but somewhere in this argument I have begun to wonder more about how her dead body would taste. How my tongue could travel from her toes to her skull, sampling every inch of the muscle beneath her husk.

How her meat would look shining from a vulture's beak. What her beautiful, dark skin would look like as the blood drained and she turned the purplish shades of lividity. Would the body blister? Would flies arrive first? If I left her in the woods where the vultures circle, would they come to me and share her? Sharing her would be the ultimate gift, the most selfless thing I could do to show the buzzards my intentions.

I imagine myself spreading black feathers from my arms and joining the vultures in their wake, their feast of the dead. A sweet togetherness as we enjoyed Luna's nutrients, honoring her before her skeleton returned to the earth.

She stands up and backs away from me, and I question if something in my gaze let her peek into my mind.

"You're a virus. You have all this rot inside you and you fill up on it until you pollute everyone around you. Then you wonder why you're alone at the end of the day with your fucking sadness and dead moths. Maybe Malik was right about you."

The pain of her last sentence strikes me harder than any other words could, than any hit across the face. The way Malik told her not to trust me. He said I was nothing more than a vain ghoul of a human who hurts people and dries them up into empty shells.

Maybe her family is dead because they couldn't fucking stand her, Luna. You ever think of that?

Malik's words play over and over in my head. The drunken slur of an argument made by a broken lover, but fuck if it doesn't sting. Maybe the pain shows on my face because a twinge of regret pulls the corners of Luna's lips down. She opens her mouth, closes it. Her hand reaches toward me, but she pulls it back like a teasing ocean tide. I wanted to drown with you Luna, not beneath you. Not away from you.

And then she turns to leave.

An unseen mass weighs within my chest and maybe that is the virus, the rot she mentioned. My own poison decaying my body from the inside out. All the angry bile souring the nectar of my heart and soul. The way death follows me, the way hostility rests inside me like a bomb coming to take comfort before detonating.

Maybe the worst part of all this is how much I like it.

The way fury fills me up, the sweet satisfaction of being a pissed off bitch to everyone and not giving a single fuck anymore. It beats complacent silence every time. The raw hatred of something, of someone else...I sit there and let it simmer. How much I hate Malik, how hurt I am at Luna's refusal to believe me, my anger toward Mr. Landon and his lies, anger at my own body for hungering for this, for all this, merely to puke it back up.

If only I could curse them all, turn them into piglets and slit them open for the turkey vultures, my brethren, to enjoy.

I have turned myself into a soured-up muck of a mess, fighting my own inclination toward the wrath my mother always knew I would succumb to. But I will try, try, try again. Teach my body to properly digest and use the carrion to sustain itself. My vision mists into red blurs and my stomach complains, demanding me to take care of my hunger for real this time. Demanding I keep down my kill.

I will understand the bitter animals who have marked me out as one of their own. I have to understand, because with Luna out the door, there is nothing left.

5

Neon red numbers glare across the clock screen on the nightstand. Strange ringing tones from my dream transition into the waking world. It's 3:00am and Mr. Landon's name glows on my cellphone's screen. He's had my cell number ever since my mom died; after all, it's only him and me out here.

Before he started telling Luna his lies about my skipping therapy sessions, he really always was a decent neighbor.

Did he see me steal the piglet?

A thin sheen of sweat sticks to my neck and forehead.

"Hello?" I answer groggily.

"You all right up there?" His normal crotchety voice is laced with notes of concern.

"Yes, why?"

"Heard something strange and the dogs have been going wild. Think a coyote got one of my pigs the other night, but now I'm thinking it might have been a person."

"Oh," I say. "Why is that?"

"A few reasons." He's being dodgy and red flags start waving in my head.

"Oh." The glow of my phone casts faint light across my bare legs tangled in the sheets. Dried blood flakes off my free hand, but

I can't find any open wounds. Maybe I flung around while sleeping and sliced my hand on the nightstand's corner.

Nothing. There are no cuts or scrapes on my skin.

Mr. Landon breaks the silence. "You sure everything is fine?"

"Yes." I swallow hard and my throat is a desert. "I'm good."

"And what about Princess Jasmine, she okay?"

I roll my eyes. Maybe he thought it was a compliment. "Do you hear how that's racist, or is it just not a factor for you?"

"Oh shush up now," he says, annoyed. "You know I ain't mean nothing by it. She okay?"

An audible sigh escapes my lips, and I put the phone on speaker to examine both hands. Dried up chips of blood dot the sheet and blankets. Two bent, black feathers are stuck to the dried blood. Vulture feathers? I'd been collecting feathers on the porch for a while now in an old wicker basket, but I don't remember going to look for more last night.

"We're both fine. She left hours ago."

"Then why's her car still at your house?"

My clammy palms and fingertips slip across the nightstand lamp as I fumble for the small switch. "Jesus, old man, none of your fucking business. She's fine."

There's a long pause and my chest tightens with an uncomfortable, warbling sensation.

"Luna's fine," I insist.

"She better be."

He hangs up and my heart plummets.

Did I hurt Luna?

I throw on a coat and some boots and run outside. Luna's cherry red car is indeed still parked in the driveway. My mind can't make sense of the vehicle's still-life existence in my yard, but I know I would never hurt her. I love her.

The blood on my hands... It has to be from another piglet. Mr.

Landon's lights are on in his house across the field. I retreat back inside and scurry into the shower. Burning drops of water scald my flesh between vigorous scrubbing. When the scarlet stains are gone, my knees give out and my body slides down the shower door. My muscles and bones protest. Tender bruises dot my arms and shins.

It was just another piglet. I fell down in the woods after taking it away from the sow. That's all. That's all....

The shower door rattles as I bang my head over and over again across the hard plastic.

Rattle-bang, rattle-bang until all the bad memories are gone. *Gurgle,* my stomach joins in on the rhythm, and we all play our bodily instruments until the overwhelming weight in my head stops pressing down.

Whatever is burbling in my gut, it stays down this time.

The living room is upturned, couch cushions strewn across the wooden floor and desk drawers pulled all the way out. There is nothing here, nothing beneath my bed or in the closets, nothing in the fridge or cabinets indicating a horrible crime or wrongdoing has been committed. Small comfort lets my lungs breathe easier for a moment, but Luna doesn't answer my calls or texts.

I leave several of each. She was so mad, maybe she walked away and called someone else to come pick her up because she didn't want to drive. She hated driving anyway. I'll call her friends, even call Malik, and see if she reached out to any of them.

Yes, that's what I do, I tell myself, hoping it isn't a lie.

After my third and final frantic voicemail to her, I crawl back into bed, wishing the panic song my heart keeps hammering out will fade away.

And it does, but only to be replaced by the clink of wind chimes echoing in my head. The same sweet melody of Luna's laugh. Dread fills me then, quick and cold like someone unlatched my jaw and shoved a hose deep into my throat. A drowning sense of utter loss floods my entire being, and I am lost beneath the water. Searching and fading, finding nothing.

—◆—

"Luna's been missing for three days," I tell Dr. Fawning.

She stares. Doesn't blink. Her tan-colored suit is splotched with black patches of *something*.

"And no, I haven't called anyone. Definitely not Malik. I think she's okay. She has to be." The woodsy scent of the office barely covers up the stench of rotten garbage. Someone needs to clean this place better.

Terror harbors itself between the curves of my rib bones, crushing me with the fear Mr. Landon will call the police soon and they will find something. I hunt frantically while awake and in the muddled memories of daydreams and nightmares, but still find nothing.

Dr. Fawning tells me to sleep more, but there are hazy gaps between the moments where I rest and wake.

The cool hardwood floor chilling my bare feet stays in my head, like I've been sleepwalking and can almost remember it. Almost. The teeth-grinding frustration of not being able to reel in an almost-memory makes me want to scream. I feel like I am going crazy.

When you've already been called crazy your entire life, there is nothing worse than thinking you are waning away into a perceived truth. If crazy becomes my truth, I don't know what else to do.

Sometimes I wake up with more feathers stuck to my skin, more dried blood on me, but just a little, never as much as that first night. What is the source? I keep hoping it's me, my own blood, but

I find no open wounds.

This morning, I woke up with an empty syringe by my pillow and I don't know where it came from or what was inside of it. I didn't tell Dr. Fawning this part yet. Did I take something? I never did illegal drugs, surprising given my inclination toward obsessions, toward addicting myself to other vices, toward a sick hunger I cannot satisfy but am so desperate to, still so desperate to understand the vultures. I am closer to finally cracking open their delicate skulls and peering at the enigmas inside...

I want to trust myself, to believe I am falling asleep and not blacking out while my body continues to conduct its movements in the dead of night without my entire cognizance.

I tell Dr. Fawning this too, and she stares back with those large, glassy eyes. She whispers to me then, makes me ask myself what I am really capable of.

What am I capable of?

The question refuses to leave my head and now Luna is gone. Every time I get closer to understanding the vultures, I lose a piece of myself along the way. Their flight, their feast, their very survival— it all circles above me in the dark forest of my mind where I have planted more graveyards than trees.

And somewhere in the darkness is my Luna, Luna, *burning bright / in the forests of the night.* My stubborn, wise girl. My fiercely, strong tiger. My eyes close and I feel her raven curls dancing between my fingers, gaze into the oaken depths of her eyes shining on a sunny day, hear the poetry of her lips pressed against my throat.

On the third night of her disappearance, the wind chimes play a ballad. Sweet, melodic laughter. The gentle clinking of her glass music echoes through the woods and entices me like a siren's song. They are a secret, calling out to me on this dark morning. It's nearly 3:00am and I have come to hate this hour, but at least I'm awake. Aware.

What saccharine horror waits, harbored in the darkness of the woods where the vultures circle? The burning darkness of the night is playing your song, Luna. Are you inviting me to sing along?

I try to ignore it, but the wind chimes grow angrier. They haunt me with screaming refrains until I sit up in the bed and scream along with them. Part of me knows it's in my head, but their song sounds so *real.* I have to go into the woods and find out. What sings to me there? Is it Luna? Does she laugh from finding her way home or cry because she is lost?

There is rage in her melody of dancing shards, rage that echoes from the fierce shaking of the trees as a winter wind howls across the fields. The nights have not been freezing cold yet, but the darkening skies promise these mild temperatures are temporary.

I think Luna shouts for me in between those violent breezes, but Dr. Fawning calls this some fancy word I can never remember, but it basically means I am *projecting* my feelings into a manifestation of noise. It is all imaginary, in my head—*"It's not real, Andi,"* my psychiatrist repeats over and over in her tan and white suits. The good doctor reminds me of a Key deer, something small and rare, found only in one area, something endangered.

"You could even make the noises go away, Andi. You're a smart girl with your whole life ahead of you, but you have to stop this obsession." Her voice sounds like mine and we blur together in the static of my thoughts, becoming one as I finally consume her, too.

Obsession means Luna. And "You're a smart girl" means *You're off your damn rocker, Andi.* She says my name too much and I say it back to myself. I wonder if she wants me to be something else, something hysterical. A bias against my own sex, but if I don't talk to her, she has no idea how much worse things could become. I love Luna like a good habit, but my obsessions remain directed toward the hunger of carrion, my need to understand the vultures as they guide me into the underworld.

I am a body learning to consume other bodies. There are no wrong bodies here when the meat is all dead and just food. I could never explain this to Dr. Fawning, and probably never to Luna.

If only Luna could see my collection of feathers now, but after the incident with the moths, I doubt this would go over well. The feathers have been relatively easy to find beneath the trees where the vultures wait, as if in caucus of where to go next, what space in the woods to circle for carrion. My bundle of black and brown, and a few tiny, white plumes, rest outside on the back porch facing away from Mr. Landon's and toward the rest of the woods. A small pile of rocks rests on the wicker basket's top to keep it safe from the wind and predators.

I have been tying the quilled ends of the feathers together with curled, black strands, admiring how they glisten in the winter's seldom sunlight. When the project is finished, I will have my own wings and fly with the great vultures and watch the world from above, waiting for life to die, to rot, to sustain me long after the living vermin of the earth are gone.

I will. I must.

Luna, return to me. Be the one to thread the wings into my back, be the one who is not afraid to make my spine bleed. But then again, maybe Luna would never be the right person. If I could convince her, I'd help her understand. I'd teach her how to eat from carcasses and collect more feathers just for her, stitch her another pair of wings to suture into her smooth flesh, too. We could fly away together.

The wind chimes refuse to stop, and it is nearly 5:00am now. My only choice is to listen.

There's something there, connected between the violent songs of glass and with Luna's disappearance. And it's not a *projection* or a *manifestation*, as my abhorrently quiet doctor would lead me into believing. She is another false prophet I keep paying to and hoping for some help in return, but I know the real messengers now. My birds, my mystical companions guarding the sky and waiting for me.

Luna-bug, my moonlight girl, keep screaming inside those wind chimes. I will find you and take you with me.

My phone vibrates against the wooden nightstand and wakes me up later in the morning. The caller isn't saved in my contacts, but I know the number. I thought about blocking him long ago, but over the years, Malik has calmed and accepted the choices of his ex-wife.

My fingers flex in hesitation, but I fear ignoring him might bring worse consequences.

"Hello?"

"Mr. Landon called me," his deep voice answers without a greeting. The pitched notes of his worry are evident.

"Is that so?" I do a terrible job of keeping the annoyance from my tone.

"He thinks you did something to Luna." Malik keeps his voice even, but the accusation still lingers, hovering over the sketchy reception.

"I love Luna." My defense.

"Oh?" he mocks me back. "She there? Put her on then."

"We had a fight. She left. All there is to it. And no, I don't know where she went so if you think you still know her so damned well why don't you figure it out." I hang up and throw my phone aside. If he texts or calls back, I don't want to know.

A rage forms in me toward Mr. Landon. Nosy bastard. I try to remember any of the techniques Dr. Fawning or my old therapist taught me for dealing with moments like this, but my brain is full of white noise and resentment, a brew for the wrath I know I'll keep drinking. If everyone would mind their own business, it would make my life a lot easier. Maybe I should be grateful so many people care about Luna and where she is. I'm sure her family and friends are worried too, but most of them don't like me and don't have my number. I'm not on social media. I'm not on anything. I am the outcast girlfriend of someone whom I do not deserve.

Maybe part of my anger stems from my jealously that everyone *cares* because if I went missing, there would only be Luna searching for me, calling my name out in the woods and from rooftops, but now I don't even have her because…because why?

I pace out into the living room and grab a couch pillow from the floor, punch it hard, command my body to stop shaking. It doesn't work, but maybe a walk will. Some cold air and perhaps a scavenger hunt for more feathers.

Or maybe take another one of the piglets just for fun and get the old farmer really wired. If he wants something to be pissed about, then fine. Let's do it. Let's fucking give him a reason.

With my boots tied and coat bundled up tightly around my shivering body, I march over to the farm and keep an eye out for Mr. Landon, but his truck isn't in the driveway. Like me, he lives alone, so if his truck is gone then he has to be, too. He must have changed his routine with the barn since the disappearance of the first piglet because the barn door is shut and locked.

I skulk around the building for another way in. My ears are alert for crunching gravel if Landon returns while I'm on his property. The barn's windows are too small for me to squeeze through, so my only option is to pick the lock or break it. I rummage through my coat pockets for a bobby pin or a pen, but a sharp jab greets me instead and scrapes against my finger.

"Ouch! What the fuck…?" I pull the twisted object from my pocket, cool and metal. The corkscrew rests in my palm near where the pointed end scratched me. I squint at it and untwist a curled black strand of hair from around the spirals.

My mind swims in a desperate, drowning wave of questions as I try to remember why the corkscrew is in my pocket. The last time I drank wine was months ago with Luna. Maybe her hair fell then and got warped in with the metal.

Luna…

No. For all I know, Mr. Landon kidnapped Luna and could be keeping her in the barn, tied up next to the sow or stowed away in the horse's stable.

My heart beats like a rabid animal trying to break free from a cage. Stinging tears threaten to spill from my eyes, but I sniffle it all away and creep back to the barn door with corkscrew in hand.

The padlock is old and rusted, and the corkscrew barely fits inside the hole. I wiggle it around and try to listen for a *click*. It takes me a good ten minutes and several failed attempts, but I pull and twist, and then kick the lock, and I curse everything in sight, and then the fucking thing finally gives in and unhooks. The door screeches open.

A warming light is still on, sitting in the corner like an overly bright witness. I walk toward the sow and she must be smarter than I give her credit for because when I approach, she goes wild. I didn't know pigs could make such a terrible noise. She's pissed. She's a mother and she knows what I did. Or she at least knows I took her baby and never brought it back.

"And I'm here to take another, you ugly bitch. I'm going to take another and eat it up, even if I vomit its bones again." Some part of my brain doesn't recognize myself after the words tumble out; it's as if I'm watching a distorted nightmare version of the woman I have become. I ache to reach out to her and silence the hunger and pain, but I don't know how.

But somewhere during this rage I have grabbed the axe from the wall of tools and am traipsing on determined feet toward the mother. Hay and dust from the ground stir up beneath my boots, leaving evidence from my trespassing. Might as well silence the mother too while I'm at it. The babies are a little bigger now with fuller bellies and wider eyes. Grunts and squeals sound out as the piglets chase and nudge each other, still sticking so close to their mother.

"I'll slaughter you all." The axe handle is smooth in my hands, a heavy comfort keeping me weighted to the ground.

"Don't you move." Mr. Landon's voice growls from the quiet day outside and I wonder how I missed hearing his truck, usually the old pickup wakes the whole forest. He walks into the barn with a shotgun pointed toward my head.

His hands tremble.

"Aww shucks, Mr. Landon," I say, imitating his accent and lowering the axe. "I ain't mean nothing by it." I give him a wink. A laugh crawls out of my throat and again, I am aware and unaware at the same time. A split-screen television of a human watching both sides of myself compete for some kind of harmony or dominance.

"Drop the axe."

The tool thuds on the dusty floor. My mouth stretches into a crooked smile.

Mr. Landon steps closer, shotgun still aimed at me, so I raise my hands in the air. *I surrender, sir.*

"What's wrong with you, girl?"

"Nothing. What's wrong with you, *man*?"

He glances at the animals and back to me. The wrinkles around his eyes grow tighter the longer he stares.

"Did you kill my pig?"

My laugh is cold even to my own ears. "Why would I kill a little piglet?"

Maybe he decides he doesn't want to know because he tells me to leave instead. "You get out of here. If I see you on my property again, I'm calling the police. Hell, might call them anyway since your girl gone missing."

"You think she's missing? Maybe *you* took Luna." I point a finger accusingly at him and shuffle closer.

"We both know that ain't true."

I keep my hands up and sidestep the axe. My head nods solemnly in agreement. "I'm real sorry, Mr. Landon. I haven't been feeling right since Luna left. I want to know she's okay."

He hesitates for a moment and lowers the gun a fraction.

I kick the axe handle forward and an unexpected pain shoots through my toe and up my leg. Wincing but determined, I lurch forward like a wild hyena. Guttural barks yip from my mouth as I spring toward him. He doesn't want to shoot me and it's all I need. My hand reaches for the weapon and I grip the handle tight. The axe *wooshes* through the air toward his arm as the old bastard decides if he really has it in him to shoot a woman or not.

A loud *crunch* emits as axe meets shoulder, and it is so exquisitely satisfying. The blood juts out and its beauty is pure poetry as the old man drops the gun, screams, and kneels on the barnyard ground. My body shivers in pleasure.

I didn't expect the axe to stick in and stay, nestled in flesh and winter coat, so I guess I need to swing harder next time. I grab the handle and really have to pull that fucker to get it out of his skinny arm.

Blood sprays me in the face and I lick at it, a glorious scarlet fountain just for me. I swing again and *hey batter, batter* I hit a home run and lop the blade neatly into his neck. His head stays attached, but those big, puffy veins spurt like a lawn sprinkler before his entire body falls face down onto the rough gravel floor.

The mother pig is really going crazy now, and she's a curious beastie. The piglets stay in their corner, but momma comes sniffing around her dead owner's blood and I cackle, feeling more gleeful than I have in months. Maybe even years.

"Lick it up!" I encourage the mother and wonder if she could develop a taste for blood and human flesh like me. Pigs are pretty trainable, after all. Maybe she could dispose of what I didn't want. If I starved her long enough, would she eat her own piglets?

Chopping Landon's body takes up the rest of my day. The dead weight is too heavy to haul into the woods alone. The vultures will appreciate the pieces of him I bring.

He severs in stringy bits, showing me the intimate ways our veins and muscles connect beneath the surface of skin and clothing. I keep a few fleshy chunks for myself, maybe to freeze and save for later because my stomach is really growling up a storm now.

I leave a few for the sow and her piglets, too. Stacking up the fresh meat in a neat stack for them to explore, hoping they taste their owner and honor him. Not that he deserves much, but what else is there to do with him? Maybe I have been too selfish throughout this whole endeavor and need to share more.

But I want most of this to be a gift for the vultures themselves, to show them how serious I am about *becoming*, my need to understand their flight, their lives, their feedings.

This man's body, my gift to them. My plea to be accepted. I am making black wings like theirs, ready to lap up blood and stain my face red like their bald heads. Ready to offer up fresh carrion for their desire, or if they'd rather let it sit, let it fester in the isolated woods until they are ready…I will watch and wait until I am ready, too.

My instructors from the Old World, from the New World, let me grow with you and adapt into the freedom of our future. I will be welcomed into their wake and we can all feast together on the body like a family. Bodies consuming bodies, nothing more.

My pile of bloodstained clothes sits in the bottom of Landon's burn barrel. The wind is strong today, howling like an angry wolf. Too strong to light the clothes on fire and turn the evidence of slaughter into ashes. Maybe tomorrow.

It's after 5:00pm by the time I've showered and cleaned up, but I've been chopping body parts since dawn, so it might as well be midnight. There's one more thing I need to do.

A blue plastic bag crinkles in my hand as I trek down the basement stairs. The moth wings are more tattered; lime green still shines from the delicate dust, but many of the patterns faded already. Carefully, I fold the wings into the bag along with the needle and thread I used to stitch them together in the first place. Maybe if Dr. Fawning sees all of this, she can help me figure something out… help fill in the missing puzzle pieces of my jigsaw brain.

Gravel crunches outside. For one wild moment I think it must be Luna, maybe a friend coming to drop her off, so she can collect her car from my driveway, but surely she will come to me first. I inhale and remember the peachy perfume, those dark strands of hair framing her strong cheekbones and fiery eyes…

I'm coming Luna—I stagger up the stairs, plastic bag in tow.

Someone knocks. Without checking through the peephole, I throw the door wide open and prepare to embrace my lover with the musical wind chime laugh.

But it is her ex-husband who stares back at me beneath the faint porch lights. He doesn't make a move to come inside. I grab a jacket from the hall tree by the door and step outside.

"What are you doing here?"

He blinks those dark eyes at me and his mouth twitches.

"Looking for Luna." The normally deep voice is quiet and cracked. This broken man who still cares so deeply for her. Something in my own chest twinges for him, a brief moment where we understand each other. The moment doesn't last long.

"What did you do, Andi?" Malik steps closer. I don't think he'd hurt me, unless I really did do something to Luna, but then I'd probably hurt myself first.

What did I do?

"I don't know," I answer. "Can't quite remember."

He walks right up to me and carefully places his big hands on my shoulders. I'm not short, but his tall, burly body demands I look up to meet his eyes. He's a beautiful man, and I wonder what he'd taste like after being dead on the road for a day or two. All that lean and strong meat strung out on the cold ground but being warmed by the sun.

They always did make a striking pair, Malik and Luna.

"Please," he says. "Please try to think."

My head shakes out a refusal.

Frustrated, he paces away in a circle on the porch, but then his eyes come to rest on something in the far corner. He walks over and points at the wicker basket. "That's Luna's. I remember it."

"She brought the basket here a year ago." I roll my eyes and try to feign some nonchalance. "It's just a decoration."

He glances at me once before kicking the rocks away from

the lid. He reaches inside and pulls out the feathers, my makeshift wings.

"Stop!" I tug at his forearm, careful not to grab the delicate feathers and undo all the work I have put into stringing my plumage together. He jerks away and slowly pulls at a chunk of the black strands holding a few of the feathers together.

"What the fuck did you do?" He looks down in horror at the strands curled between his fingers.

"Nothing! Give them back." *My wings, my freedom.* "Please."

He looks like he'd rather stab the feathers through my eyes. "This…it's Luna's hair." The black knots come undone as he tugs at the curled strands. A bundle forms in his palm like a midnight nest. Staring at the almost complete set of wings and then back at me, a look of disgust passes over his face before he chucks the wings away like they burned him. They fall softly onto the concrete as the breeze catches the feathers and tosses them around the porch.

"You're sick."

My feathers. Luna's hair chopped off and looped together like strands of thread holding the quills together. *You were always essential, Luna-bug. My tether to the world.* My eyes squeeze tightly shut while Malik huffs out another stream of angry words.

Luna's anger—how she ran from the bathroom door and out into the driveway. I followed her, intent on chasing her down the lane, but she was sitting in the car, too upset to drive.

She got out after I started pounding on the windshield and we talked. We fought again about the same things. She called me a freak and the pain of those words spilled into my chest like lava, disintegrating my heart.

"I love you, Luna. I love you so much. I want to know what every part of you tastes like. What's wrong with that?" I remember saying.

"I sacrificed so much for you. I left my husband when I realized I was in love with you. My family nearly abandoned me over leaving

71

my nice little normal marriage for some bony ass white girl, and you meant everything to me, Andi. And now you're freaking me the hell out with your weird shit! Every year there's been something…those fucking moths. Now blood? It's too much."

I hated the terror on her face, but I didn't know what to say. The hurt and the wrath, bubbling into a tar of resentment. The vultures circling overhead, whispering to me. How she reduced me to this weird stranger and nothing more.

"I don't feel good," I say to Malik.

He raises a thick eyebrow in concern, probably more so for Luna's sake than mine. "You need some meds or something? Want to go inside?"

"No, I need my therapist. I need to talk to her."

"Andi, Luna is—"

"Missing. I know! Jesus, Malik. Of course I fucking know. I just, I don't feel good. I have to go to Dr. Fawning now. I have to talk to her." Keys jangle inside my jacket as I stumble over a rock on the way to my car.

"Andi."

"Fucking don't." I fling the driver's side door open and place the bag in the backseat. "If you want me to remember, I have to go now." *Have to go, have to go….*

Have to see her. Dr. Fawning with her big doe eyes and her silly suits and I have to talk to her. Need to know, need to remember what I did. She always listens; she'll listen now and I will figure this out.

Malik slides himself into the passenger seat. He's still talking. Words go in, but they don't process. I am one-track-minded. I am in need. I need to finish the wings and sew them onto my back and fly away from all of this, fly into the sky and circle with my kettle of vultures.

Dead or alive, I will find my wind chime girl.

Honor her.

Here I go, here we go, here we fly. I am flying down the driveway and a man is talking to me from my passenger seat, but I have to get to the office, have to crawl through the undergrowth of her hidden space and find Dr. Fawning and make her *tell me* what is happening. Make her talk aloud and not just in my fucking head.

My car bumps along and the man yells. Dying sunlight glints off the metallic edges of Landon's rooftop. Shining like the corkscrew I grabbed off the counter before chasing Luna down.

My nighttime cocktail of the wine I wasn't supposed to drink and stolen meds and Robitussin, all my sleep aids fusing a Molotov bomb inside me, these things I tried so hard to stay away from, and *what was in the syringe, Andi?*

I don't know, but the corkscrew was so cold and slick resting against my palm. It was sparkly, like it had been recently washed when I found it before breaking into Mr. Landon's barn.

Before…I curled my hand hard around it and when I finally had her down, when she ran into the woods and screamed at my sanctuary, I drove the corkscrew deep into Luna's thighs, untapping her blood and letting it pool into my mouth. Her sweet red wine, all mine. She refused to give it to me, so I took it on my own. She kicked and fought, she bruised my ribs with her foot, but she didn't understand how powerful my need was.

I had to taste her.

How do I make them understand this? How do I make them understand what it is like to live with this hungry beast so deep inside your soul? My beast, a vulture, demanding carrion, come to roost inside me and so powerful, so vast in its presence of great wings. For once, the other demons who dance in my mind's graveyard have been silent. They watched in awe at the vultures. I thought if I became one of them, if I learned to fly and feast and circle the world in silent gestures, perhaps all the love I buried these past twenty-some years would grant me peace.

I did not count on there being an even greater beast waiting inside, simmering me alive; I am the daughter of wrath, and to wrath I shall return.

I don't want to remember Luna's screams when I gashed open her thighs. How the corkscrew slashed through her hair, ripped it away in savage tufts as she was knocked down.

The way the syringe slid into her so easily. As easily as my fingers when she was panting for me, when she wanted me. She'd never want me again.

"Andi," she had cried. "Please, stop. Help me."

HelpHelpHelp and then the serene quiet of the cold woods and the beauty of the vultures circling above us.

No, she's not dead yet. And she's mine. I cannot share her with you. I know I promised, but I love her too much to share.

Maybe that's what Dr. Fawning meant by my obsession.

The metal honey of her blood, such a delicacy in my mouth, swirling around my tongue. I used the corkscrew to saw off the tiniest morsels of flesh. It was chewier than the dead piglet and bloodier, but it was *Luna,* and I knew I'd crave her whole body soon. I needed her to die slowly, beautifully...

Have to talk to Dr. Fawning. Have to fix this.

I arrive at her office and put the car in park before switching the engine off.

"What are you doing?" the man says.

I turn to the man and wonder why he is in my car. "I have to talk to my doctor. She's waiting. She's going to be mad. I don't have an appointment today, but I think she'll still hear me out because it's urgent."

Earth crunches beneath my boots, and the blue plastic bag contrasts harshly with the dull brown of the wintery world outside. Cold dirt and scattered twigs line my way into the office. Maybe the air fresheners are gone because a rank and sour odor pervades my senses, heavier than before. The sky darkens overhead the way it does in winter, promising early night, but I have been here enough times, I don't need an abundance of light to navigate my way through.

"Dr. Fawning?" I call. She is the singular presence here. Ever. No other staff or secretaries. Only the doctor with her big eyes and tan suits.

She answers me quietly and I kneel, taking my seat in the dirt. The wind whistles a sad, winter tune and the man gags behind me.

"Shh," I say and stare him down, remembering his name. "Malik, this is a private session, please wait outside."

"We *are* outside. What the fuck is this?"

I sigh. Annoyed. "Whatever." I turn toward Dr. Fawning and try to figure out where to start. Patient as ever, she waits.

"I think I hurt Luna. I just wanted to understand the vultures. They've been following me. Did they want me to become part of their wake? Were we meant to feast together? I tried to bring them Luna, but didn't want to share her, so I brought them Mr. Landon instead. They liked him. I think once I finish my wings I can go home with them."

Dr. Fawning is quiet, but she watches me. She listens.

"But I'm afraid, doctor. I'm afraid they'll make me share Luna or not accept me at all. It isn't fair."

Malik gags behind me again. "I'm calling the cops, Andi." He hurries away with his cellphone and I wish him luck finding reception out here.

Dr. Fawning and I continue to stare at one another. She whispers to me and I nod. Her ears are gone, and her nose is shriveled and brown like a rotting mushroom. The eyes are still exquisite. Big and full of glossy wonder.

The trees rustle but do not carry Luna's wind chime tune. The lack of her laughter, her screams, her moans…it makes the woods emptier. I need to hear the wind chimes sing between the naked branches and guide me to her because I have forgotten—tried to hide her from the vultures, hid her from myself along the way.

Luna, my love song, my tiger in the forest. I want to apologize. I want to swallow you whole.

"They're coming." Malik returns and the dead leaves swirl around his feet when the wind replies instead of me.

"Dr. Fawning, I don't want to go to jail. All I have ever wanted is freedom. Please don't let them take my life from me."

A bird in a cage, a great big buzzard never allowed to circle and find food, to feel the exhilaration of air dancing through my wings. I can't live behind bars and eat cooked scraps. I refuse.

"Jesus, Andi. Stop it!" Malik paces closer and his face is skewed up in disgust and fear more than anger. "Stop talking to that fucking *thing*."

"Luna never talked to me like such a jerk." I glare at him.

"Yeah, well, where the hell is she, huh?" He is nearly crying now, and I think he should talk to Dr. Fawning about his emotions, so I tell him so because she really is a wonderful listener.

He shakes his head, his mouth open in a dumb confusion. "I'm not talking to a dead deer in the middle of the woods. Look at it! Why is it suspended from the tree? Who hangs up their kill in the woods and leaves it there to rot?"

He turns to me now. "Luna said you weren't going to your sessions. Is *this* what you've been doing?"

Malik's exasperation fills the air. Betrayal and fury sink deep into my heart and lungs like a deadly snake bite, knocking the breath from my lips. How could Luna have told Malik about these private things between us?

A rasping moan rings out from beneath a pile of overgrowth, twigs, and dead leaves. A broken wind chime of a noise, directing itself into my chest and tearing me apart. The haze fades from my eyes and I stare at Dr. Fawning in front of me. She shifts in and out of focus between being the woman in a tan suit with a white undershirt and a big dead doe, hanging from her hind legs off a sturdy branch. I try to merge the two in my head, but the painful moaning continues. The wind carries it in all directions around the forest. Malik is shouting and taking off in the wrong direction.

The vultures circle above, and a few hang out on the highest branches, an execution committee, waiting and judging.

My Dr. Fawning stops whispering, and instead her maggots and flies murmur from their nestled bed deep inside her slashed belly. Most of the insect activity has stopped, but a few remain, trying to suck away the last of their sustenance from the deer's body. The exposed liver and lungs sit like islands in a watery accumulation of where the insides have liquified through their active decay. The fur, my doctor's suit, is matted and wet; the pungent odor sours the air in a curdle of putrid perfumes.

I shuffle closer to the undergrowth and brush away twigs and dirt from a bleeding head with chunks of hair missing. Luna's eyes struggle to open beneath the caked mud over her face. The soil is stubborn, but some of it brushes away when I kiss her forehead. Her blue-tinged lips tremble.

"Luna," I whisper, "I'm going to take care of you. I'm going to honor you."

"Help me. Please." She cries and crawls out of the undergrowth toward the clearing. "Ouch! Fuck."

Her palm comes down on a jagged rock and scrapes the skin away. Her other hand is wrapped in a piece of the blanket I left her with. She tied it tightly, but the way her other fingers have turned into a charcoal gray tells me frostbite has not been kind.

I help move her away from the rocks and sit her up against the trees where Dr. Fawning sways in the winter wind.

"See? I never stopped going to my sessions. I didn't lie," I say and beam at her, proud to show her my truths. "Dr. Fawning always listens."

Luna dry heaves and throws her body backward, away from the doctor and away from me. I follow and straddle her, grabbing her freshly cut palm to lick the blood and dirt away. She cries out and tries to buck me off, but I can tell it hurts too much. Every movement is a new wave of pain to her, a new nightmare. I have to set her free.

My hands stretch toward the bag, barely in reach. Luna squawks beneath me as I wrestle her coat off and tear open the back of her sweater. Toned hazelnut skin swells beneath my fingertips.

"I'm sorry," I say. "You should have just taken the gift, Luna."

Her weak body writhes and jerks between sobs. The needle threads with ease from my practiced hands. Tattered moth wings wait on the forest floor, as if eager for a new host. My Luna, we must be free together. Our becoming is joined, intimately linked.

A scream tears from her throat as the sharp needle slips beneath her skin. "The thread is lime," I tell her. "Like your eyeshadow. Like the wings when they were fresh."

Blood jewels in thick drops from her back, raining down into the thread and moth dust.

"Please stop." Her cries echo into the woods.

My heart breaks, but she needs to suffer to transform. "The metamorphosis is never easy, Luna-bug. Not for us."

She stills but her breath quickens. My hands work faster, securing half of the Luna moth wings along her spine. Her skin ripples with each jab of the needle.

Leaves crunch beneath Malik's shoes as he circles back from the opposite direction he ran in.

I shuffle off Luna, avoiding her wounded thighs where I have cut and chewed. The rags I wrapped around her leg weren't tied very well, but at least she hasn't bled to death yet.

"Go away!" I shout and turn toward him, needing to be alone with Luna and complete my gift to the vultures—the gift to myself because even though it kills me inside, I know I will never be free until I share the song in Luna's blood with the buzzards. They have fallen in love with her just as I did. But when it's all done, we will fly together. A family.

There is a gray blur in the corner of my eye as Luna lurches forward and grabs something from the ground. I move my head back toward her, but a hot, sharp pain collides with my temple and slides its way down my spine like the vibrations of a ringing bell.

Agony seizes my bones and I collapse, curling up on the forest floor as my breath staggers from my lungs.

"Fuck you, Andi!" Luna shrieks and crawls away. Somewhere in my burning haze, I am surprised at this burst of strength she has managed to retain. All her anger, her need to hurt me back, she saved energy up for me. My stunning girl, my fearsome tigress of a human, you have the wrath, too. How dare you try to deny it?

I reach a hand toward her ankle and graze her with my nails, but the throbbing in my head is so bad from the pointed rock I can't properly judge my hand-eye coordination. Tears from the pain swell up in my eyes and warm blood runs down my face from the sharp cut. Luna tries to stand but stumbles back down next to me. Her eyes meet mine for a sweet moment and I die inside from the way my love for her blossoms up again and again, always.

"I love you, Luna-bug." My fingers stretch toward her. She blinks and then reaches a hand around behind her.

Pain winces across her dirt-smeared face, and she screams as she tears the needle from her back with the hand that isn't frostbitten. She heaves her body toward me. The needle connects with my cheek, sliding through flesh with eye-watering pain, going all the way through to graze my teeth.

Luna's fingers refuse to work any longer. They are dead after a final act of strength. She screams out into the woods and uses her elbows to crawl away.

My stubborn love, fighting to the end. I watch from a daze as she finally accepts Malik's help and he hobbles away with her out of the forest. I wonder if they will stumble across Mr. Landon's remains, or if they will even recognize what I have done to him.

I wonder if they will scream.

Malik might be able to get Luna help in time, but she lost a lot of blood, and I gave her a lot of drugs. She's lucky the nights didn't freeze over more, or perhaps one day I would have stumbled down and removed the dirt and twigs and blankets I buried her body under to find a frozen Luna waiting to be pecked at by the birds. By me. I could have surrounded her body with foliage and built her green wings like the moths. She'd like the bright color much better than the dark wings of the vultures.

But she didn't freeze, no, not my girl. Always burning bright. "*In the forests of the night…*" I recite the poem as the sirens approach in a prolonged wail beyond the woods. Luna was the tiger to my lamb, always fiercer and more self-assured than me, but wrath planted fangs inside this lamb. Planted an insatiable hunger for freedom.

The sirens near Mr. Landon's place and quiet. Malik doesn't even peek over his shoulder as he helps carry the bloody and limp Luna in his arms. A final glimpse of the wilted wings hanging partially sewn on her back grants me a small warmth. Halfway to freedom, my girl.

My hand shakes as I yank the needle out, sending fresh waves of hot pain to spike through my face. Blood pulls both inside my mouth and on the outside of my cheek, warm and coppery.

"I'm so sorry, Luna," I sob to the trees, to Dr. Fawning. No one else is listening. No one else has ever dared to listen.

I have nowhere to run and no one to run to. The horrific sting still throbs down my whole body like I've been beaten over with a cinder block. The ambulance sirens are joined with police lights just beyond the tree lining. I crawl toward the lights, toward Luna, and then stop as Dr. Fawning watches on.

"I'm sorry, Dr. Fawning, but I can't go to jail. I refuse."

She entrances me forward and I crawl to the place where her heart once beat. Long, dark lashes frame the doe eyes full of promise. My stomach snarls inside, rattling my body with angry, starving teeth.

If I can't fly away with the birds, I will settle for being another body they consume. Perhaps they will honor me, praise my skeleton and liquifying organs as I return to the earth as we all must. As we all deserve to do and nothing more.

Dr. Fawning's split body is centimeters away. I breathe in the rank and familiar scent of decay, letting the rancid meat waft its promises through my body, letting my stomach know what is coming so I don't throw it all back up. I can't. Not this time, or else I will never be free. The small pieces I stole from Luna's body, I never vomited back up. It grants me peace, to know I will keep part of her inside me, always.

My lips tremble and hesitate for a moment before I see the vultures soaring closer. Their great wings weave around the naked branches of all these bald trees that separate my property from the now dead Mr. Landon's. I left him for them, but the birds hiss at me—telling me to commit to them, prove myself once and for all. If I can meet their expectations, they will show me how to become satisfied with hunger, how to live my next life as a carrion bird because this life has consumed me whole.

Dr. Fawning's matted fur brushes sweetly against my lips. I lurch forward as the sirens stop. A cop calls out my name from the edge of the trees, but my mouth is full of the doe's sour meat. I chew down on a sliver of decomposing intestine that's nearly frozen. My teeth crack but a small burst of juices escapes. They flavor my taste buds in the skunked rottenness from the doe's body.

Liquid slides down my throat, purging me, and the vultures scream overhead. Their wings bat the air, encouraging me to become like them, like I have always been.

A sour human too discontent in her obsessions and addictions to want anything real in this life. Even Luna couldn't save me.

Fouled meat piles into my mouth, raw and barely chewed. I keep stuffing it in even as I gag from suffocation, needing the venison to choke me until death's darkness claims my body for the underworld. Some of it slides down into my grumbling stomach, but I hold as much of the gooey flesh between tongue and throat as possible. I will stuff myself full of carrion until I build a dam between my airway. A body consuming another body, sharing it with flies and maggots who have come to dance on my tongue and smear against the roof of my mouth.

My neck darts forward again, and I peck at the deer, trying to devour what I can between the rib cages. Some bones have broken away and I tear at the blackened mass that used to be Dr. Fawning's heart. The bones scrape my cheeks and poke at my forehead. I close my eyes and dive into the decayed body as far as I can, stuffing my cheeks until I asphyxiate.

I am like the vultures, gorging myself on this carcass; a feast meant solely for me and the insects who have come to live inside my doctor. The vultures circle overhead, out of reach. Watching, but never joining in.

Accept me, I beg.

Above me, they still reign, but if they would come down, maybe I could be their queen for a moment, the queen of vultures—feast with me, my beautiful birds. Join me in this wake before I die.

The meat and juices and squelched maggots all coagulate inside my mouth, bulging out my cheeks with their smashed decay. I refuse to swallow it down as the cops blur into my vision from behind the trees. The gray skies open and fat flakes of snow descend upon us all—perhaps Mr. Landon's promised winter storm at last.

My throat clenches and tries to force the meat out. I slap a hand over my mouth and keep the deer's putrid flesh stuck there, killing me on the carrion I so hungered for. Freezing gusts tear through my coat, but the chill helps keep my composure, helps keep the dead meat inside my body.

My freedom though, it's all I ever wanted. I will not become a bird behind their cages. I refuse. Yes, something will be dead here, nestled between the trees separating my property from Mr. Landon's. Something is already dead and maybe the birds knew I would come here all along. Maybe they saved Dr. Fawning for this moment. I imagine one final grave within the cemetery I've constructed inside my head. Here, my perceived wrongness dissipates. Here, I am a body consuming another body, waiting for the carrion birds to finish us all. Waiting for the snow to cover the balding earth and offer a false promise of clean beauty.

There has never been such a thing.

They are all so bitter, just like me. Luna, Malik, the cops, even dead Mr. Landon. And my parents, how they should have survived for me. My father's bitterness ruining us all. *I am the daughter of wrath.*

All creatures of habit desperately in search of something they will never find.

My eyelids flutter and I picture the image of my mother's beautiful, ruined eyes reflected back at me from Dr. Fawning's putrefied head. Crystal blue drowned in ice, in blood.

I found what I wanted and needed, though the vultures still orbit above like unobtainable black stars. Beautiful and from another world. I should have known better.

I found my freedom even if it comes at the cost of such a suffocating, vehement end.

But at least it is my ending, my bitter devouring. At least it is something they cannot take from me.

Shimmering Luna Moth

— ◆ —

Ingredients

1.5oz Midori
1oz Vodka
1oz Triple Sec
.5oz Simple syrup
.5oz Lemon juice
1oz Pineapple juice
Lemon lime soda
Silver edible glitter

Instructions

1. Add ice to a glass
2. In a cocktail shaker, combine Midori, vodka, Triple Sec, simple syrup, lemon juice, and pineapple juice
3. Shake thoroughly
4. Pour into glass filled with the ice
5. Add edible glitter, top with lemon lime soda
6. Stir and watch the way the glitter shimmers, just like the delicate wings of a beloved Luna moth…

Recommendation: For the ice, try freezing fresh mint leaves into ice cubes. You want to feel connected to the earth, don't you? Andi would want you to—so would the vultures, and they're watching. Remember, they're always watching.

Shimmering Luna Moth (mocktail)

Instructions

1. For a mocktail version, try freshly brewed green tea!
2. Let tea cool, and then shake with .5oz simple syrup, .5oz lemon juice, and 1oz pineapple juice
3. Pour into glass filled with the ice
4. Add edible glitter, top with lemon lime soda (I know it sounds odd with tea, but try it!)
5. And as above, stir and watch the glitter shimmer as you ponder making yourself a nice pair of Luna moth wings

Note: If you enjoy matcha tea, you can substitute it for the green tea or make a green tea and matcha blend (one of my favorites!). Matcha adds that extra earthiness for an even stronger bond with the circling vultures…

Author Acknowledgements

I remain incredibly grateful to so many people who have supported my twisted little novella over the years. I will surely forget some names, but please know much every review, share, tweet, video, and everything has meant and continues to mean to me. It all matters.

I'm so thrilled to be working with Apocalypse Party Press for the book's resurrection. All of my thanks to Ben DeVos and his incredible work and enthusiasm.

I have to give a special thanks to Hailey Piper, Sam Brunke-Kervin, Gwendolyn Kiste, Jonathan Janz, Christa Carmen, Mike Arnzen, Cassie Daley, Corey Niles, Megan Matejcic-Benson, the Horror Spotlight team who granted *To Be Devoured* the LOHF 2019 award for Best Novella, Dilatando Mentes Editorial, and the Staring Into the Abyss podcast who did two really fun discussions on *To Be Devoured,* (thank you, Richard, Matt, and Villimey!). I'm so thankful for you all, for your friendship, and for your support of my first novella.

And an extra special thanks to the talented Red Lagoe for her beautiful foreword. Red, your support and kind words are so, so appreciated.

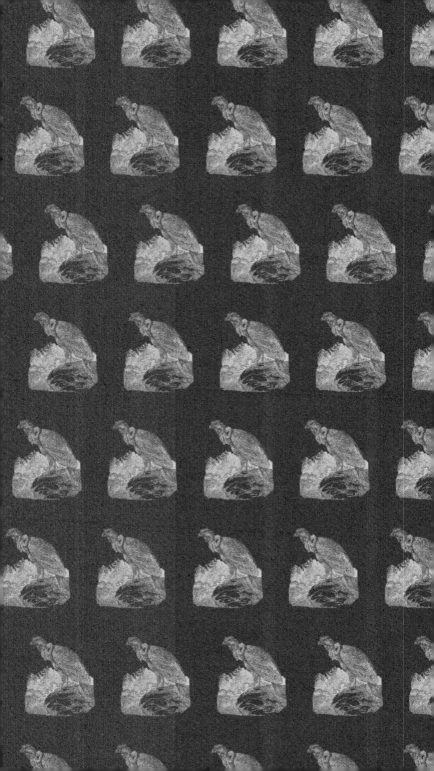

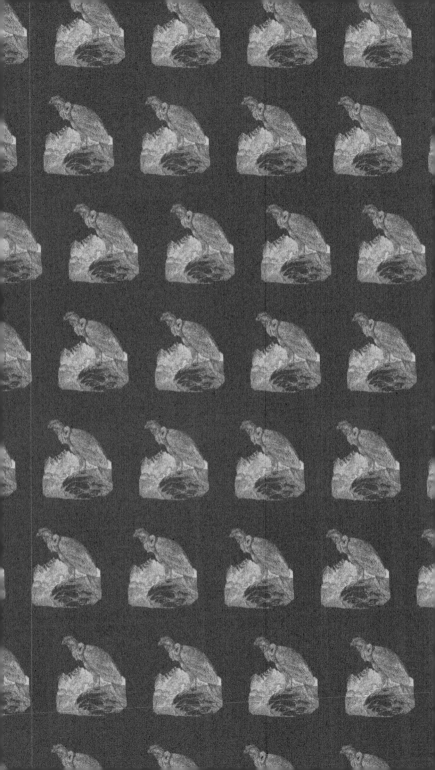